BRUNCH AT THE ALL ALIEN CAFE

SHORT FICTION FROM THE ENTANGLED UNIVERSE

MARY E. LOWD

"The Little Red Avian Alien" © 2014 by Mary E. Lowd. First published in *Luna Station Quarterly, Issue 020*.

"Winged Folk Only" © 2018 by Mary E. Lowd. First published in *Daily Science Fiction*.

"Go High" © 2018 by Mary E. Lowd. First published in *Daily Science Fiction*.

"I Am Mazillion" © 2020 by Mary E. Lowd. First published in *All Worlds Wayfarer, Issue IV: Vernal Equinox*.

"Hidden Feelings" © 2015 by Mary E. Lowd. First published in *Daily Science Fiction*.

"Hidden Intentions" © 2017 by Mary E. Lowd. First published in *Analog: Science Fiction and Fact, March/April 2017 Issue*.

"Green Skin Deep" © 2020 by Mary E. Lowd. First published in *All Worlds Wayfarer, Issue VI: Autumnal Equinox*.

"Many Tiny Feet" © 2017 by Mary E. Lowd. First published in *New Myths, Issue 40*.

"Where the Heart Is" © 2011 by Mary E. Lowd. First published in *Stories of Camp RainFurrest*.

"Welcome to Ob'glaung" © 2019 by Mary E. Lowd. First published in *Midwest Furfest 2019 Conbook*.

"One Alien's Wreckage" © 2017 by Mary E. Lowd. First published in *Daily Science Fiction*.

"The Crowds on Crossroads Station" © 2017 by Mary E. Lowd. First published in *Daily Science Fiction*.

"Principles Over Profit" © 2017 by Mary E. Lowd. First published in *Daily Science Fiction*.

"Inalienable Rights" © 2017 by Mary E. Lowd. First published in *Daily Science Fiction*.

"Crescent Horns and Tall Ears" © 2017 by Mary E. Lowd. First published in *Daily Science Fiction*.

For Douglas Adams, P. G. Wodehouse, and my mom who let me carry her copy of The World of Mr. Mulliner around in my backpack until it was all beaten up and gave me Mostly Harmless for my birthday.

With special thanks to Eric Witchey for teaching me skills and strategies that nearly tripled my writing speed and led to the existence of so many of these stories.

CONTENTS

WELCOME TO MY UNIVERSE

A UNIVERSE IS a big and complex place, and there's only ever time for an individual to enjoy a small slice of it. Each slice is different—some have more crust, some have more filling. To some the slice tastes sweet with a lingering aftertaste; for others, the flavors are more mixed—bitter, sour, and sweet in turn.

In this book, you will find an array of morsels selected from the buffet of my space opera universe. Characters recur, and settings overlap. You'll meet exciting alien species and visit beautiful, faraway places. Sometimes, you get to glimpse pieces of the same story through different sets of eyes, understanding it from a new angle. The stories—like the eyes many are seen through—are multi-faceted.

Perhaps, there are some flavors you'll prefer to others; some dishes you'll like more than the rest. But altogether, this selection of tastes comes together to make a full, hearty, well-rounded and satisfying meal.

So please, join me for brunch at the All Alien Cafe.

1

———

THE LITTLE RED AVIAN ALIEN

IT WAS Avian Night at the All Alien Cafe. The avian population of Crossroads Station wasn't large, but they were vocal and social. The double winged Eechies and the puff-feathered Rennten could always be counted on to attend, since they'd evolved as colony dwellers. However, occasionally, even a traditionally solitary, long-legged Ululu would show up and regale the crowd with stories of how his people had built high-pressure nests inside all the gas giants in a thirty light-year radius of Crossroads Station before humans even noticed them.

Avian Night always had a good turnout.

Prilla was a puffy, auburn feathered Rennten. She always came for the drink specials, but she stayed for the commiserating chatter. Humans and the other mammalian races simply didn't understand what it was like to be a hatched race. They didn't understand the pressures of incubating external ovum nor the intense ambivalence of being a flighted species living on a space station. *To fly higher than the stars! Yet to be trapped, always, inside an enclosed building...* Mind-boggling.

That evening, however, the conversation drifted toward homeworld recipes. As Prilla listened to the others chatter, her nostrils were flooded with the remembered smell of her own favorite fledgling food: her hatch-mother's grassberry crepelettes.

The very next day, Prilla decided that she would get some grassberry seeds and grow her own grassberry plant in the arboretum on Crossroads Station. When the grassberries ripened, she'd be able to cook grassberry crepelettes of her own!

THE FIRST STEP was to catch a flight to her homeworld, several systems over, and find some grassberry seeds. Prilla went to her friend, Yss the reptilian Srellick, who ran a cargo route between Crossroads Station and the asteroid belt. She owned her own ship.

Yss was lounging in front of the airlock berth to her cargo ship. She'd set up a pair of folding chairs, a parasol, and a sunlamp. The green scales on her tail glittered in the flood of light; the parasol shaded the rest of her body. Her eyes were hidden by techno-glasses that were likely streaming data in front of her eyes on their tiny, shaded screens.

"Yss," Prilla said, "I have decided to fly to my homeworld and get the seeds for a grassberry plant, so I can grow it in the arboretum here. When the grassberries ripen, I can harvest them and make my own grassberry crepelettes for everyone to try and share!"

Yss's long tongue flickered out of her mouth. "Grassberry crepelettes?" she hissed. "Yes, that sounds nice. Do sit down, and we can eat them together."

"No, no," Prilla said. "You don't understand. I need to fly to my homeworld first to get the seeds. Will you take me? On your ship?"

Yss's tongue flickered again. Prilla could see its forked tip.

Yss continued to stare in her direction, her eyes hidden by the techno-glasses. Finally, she said, "No, I'm too busy."

Prilla began to ask, "What are you busy with? A cargo run to the asteroids?" But there was no need to ask. It was readily apparent that Yss was between cargo runs. She simply didn't want to help. Prilla's feathers ruffled in irritation, but when she opened her beak, she said, "Fine. I'll book a commercial flight and travel to my homeworld to get the grassberry seeds myself."

The lenses of Yss's techno-glasses stared blankly at Prilla as the little Rennten shuffled away.

COMMERCIAL SPACELINER TICKETS WERE EXPENSIVE, and the two day flight to her homeworld was long and tedious without a friend to share it. When she arrived, however, Prilla was delighted to be back at her childhood home. She stretched her wings and flew as she had not done in years. She visited her old hatch-den, ran into several Rennten she'd known as a fledgling, and stocked up on many familiar supplies from her childhood. Including the small yet precious bag of grassberry seeds.

By the time Prilla finished the return flight to Crossroads Station, she was itching to begin growing the grassberry seeds.

She sought out her friend Antari in the arboretum. Antari was a fishlike alien, light enough to float in the Crossroads Station atmosphere but who needed to wear a breathing helmet there to survive. He was in charge of the largest communal arboretum on Crossroads Station. Prilla found him drifting, eight feet above the ground, among several flowering trees in the Ancient Earth section. His delicate blue fins draped gracefully as he examined the health of the plants under his stewardship.

"Antari!" Prilla clacked from her beak. "I have grassberry seeds here from my homeworld! I want to plant a patch of them, and when the grassberries ripen I can make grassberry crepelettes for us all to share!"

Antari floated down, closer to Prilla's eye-level. He held out his fins, and Prilla offered him the bag of seeds. He examined the seeds closely and asked Prilla many questions about the plant ecology of her homeworld. After an exhaustive discussion of bio-dynamics and all cleverly different ways that life had evolved chlorophyll on different planets, Prilla found herself growing quite frustrated.

"Antari," she said, "I'm happy to discuss this with you at a later time, but, for now, I want to get these seeds planted. Will you help me?"

Antari bobbled up and down in the air, filling and emptying his swim-bladder much as if he were breathing heavily. "Well," he said, in a voice made deep and resonant by the amplifiers in his breathing helmet, "The truth is that this arboretum is very carefully balanced. We can't just plant one grassberry bush. Now, if you can get me an entire array of seeds from your homeworld, a complete cross-section of a self-sustaining eco-system, if you will..."

Antari never got to finish. Prilla clacked her beak in irritation, and said, "Never mind. I'll get a pot and plant the seeds in my own quarters."

"Yes," Antari intoned. "That would probably be best."

Prilla clutched the precious bag close and left the arboretum for the merchant quarter. She found a shop that that carried lovely ceramic pots and mineral-rich potting soil. She planted the seeds herself and placed the terracotta pot proudly by the inside wall, just next to her quarters' front door.

AFTER HER VACATION to her homeworld, Prilla found herself behind at work. She worked in the Robotic Sentience Offices, and the requests from robots to be evaluated for sentience had stacked up while she was gone.

"Oh dear," Prilla said, as she scanned through all the messages on her computer screen. "I'll have to schedule so many sentience tests this week that I won't be able to make it back to my quarters at lunch to water my grassberry bush each day."

Aniel turned her metallic head and made a sympathetic sound. She was one of the robots who had passed the sentience tests and, with her newfound freedom, had chosen to work in the Robotic Sentience Offices, helping to liberate other enslaved robots.

"Would you mind going to my quarters and watering my grassberry bush for me during lunches this week?" Prilla asked her robotic co-worker hopefully.

The irises in Aniel's mechanical eyes narrowed.

"I know you don't eat," Prilla said. "So, it will be less of an inconvenience for you. Though, oh dear... I suppose that means you won't want to share the grassberry crepelettes with me when they're done..."

Aniel had been listening to Prilla chatter on about the virtues of grassberry crepelettes all morning. This was the first that Prilla had remembered that her co-worker couldn't eat them.

"I am perfectly capable of enjoying a social get-together where my biological companions share food," Aniel said in a measured tone.

Prilla clapped her feathered hands happily. "Oh, good!" she said.

Heedless, Aniel continued on: "However, I have already devoted my lunch hours this week to another cause."

The feathers on Prilla's neck ruffled, and she had to take her hands and smooth them. "Is that so?" she clucked, skeptically.

Aniel insisted that it was. Though, no matter how much

Prilla tried to tease the exact nature of this *other cause* out of her, Aniel remained evasive.

Prilla skipped her lunches that week, hurrying back to her quarters during the brief break she had between scheduled sentience tests to water her grassberry bush. It was a hungry week, but it only served to whet her appetite for grassberry crepelettes.

As THE WEEKS turned into months, the grassberry bush grew strong and leafy. Prilla found it to be a valued reminder of home on a gleaming, metal space station filled with strange aliens who didn't seem to value her friendship as much as she thought they had. Or the prospect of grassberry crepelettes.

When the time came to harvest the grassberries, Prilla made one last attempt to interest one of her closest friends in taking part in her journey of reminiscence. She invited Ryeh, a canine alien with thick, flowing black fur to meet her at the All Alien Cafe. The two of them enjoyed meeting for drinks together and watching the humans in the cafe give them odd looks. There was something about a pair of aliens who looked like a big black wolf and a little red hen, drinking together, that always gave those funny smooth-skinned primates a moment of pause.

"Ryeh," Prilla explained after their second round of marzi-cran sherries, "I'm going to harvest my grassberries tomorrow and make crepelettes! There's enough berries to cook up a feast, and I'd like you to come help me cook it and eat it."

Ryeh was a quiet sort, so it didn't worry Prilla when it took her a minute to answer. Her answer, however, was less than satisfactory.

"I don't cook," Ryeh said.

Prilla was flabbergasted. Having her final friend turn her

down almost pushed her into an early molting. She spent the rest of the evening arguing with Ryeh, but apparently her canine friend had suffered some horrible cooking disaster in her formative years. She would not budge.

"Fine," Prilla said. "I'll cook the crepelettes myself." *And,* she thought, *I'll eat them myself too.*

THE NEXT DAY WAS A HOLIDAY, and Prilla didn't have to go in to work. She had the whole day to herself to pluck the grassberries from the bush, which had grown all the way to the ceiling of her small quarters; blanch the berries in boiling water and peel away their waxy skin; cook them in a savory sauce; and, finally bake them into the flaky, crusty crepelettes.

She set the table beautifully, even taking time to put a bouquet of grassberry leaves in the center. However, when she sat down to her giant feast, she found that her resolve failed her. She couldn't eat a feast like this, meant to be shared, all alone. She began to wonder if she really belonged living on a space station like Crossroads, or, perhaps, whether she should move back to her homeworld.

Then Prilla heard the chime of the front door to her quarters. When she answered it, Prilla found Ryeh, Antari, Yss, and even Aniel standing there.

Prilla's feathers puffed out, turning her into a fluffy, angry, little ball of red feathers. She looked up at her *so-called friends,* ready to give them a thorough hen-pecking, a real piece of her mind, for expecting to share in the bounty of her grassberry crepelettes after each and every one of them had refused to help her with them.

Before she could speak, however, Yss held out a bottle of Almachian wine in her green scaly hands. "I traded for this on my latest asteroid run from an Almach wine baron," she hissed. "I thought it would go well with your grassberry crepelettes."

Prilla blinked. She wanted to be mad, but she knew how rare Almachian wine was. She'd always wanted to try some, but, without the necessary network of contacts, it was nearly impossible to come by. She held out her feathered hands and took the bottle from Yss's scaly ones. Yss stepped past her through the door and seated herself at the feast-laden table.

Prilla stayed standing squarely in the way of the others though, meaning to give each of them a tongue-lashing, even if Yss had bought her way out of it.

Antari, however, held forward a bowl filled with brightly colored, gem-like globes of fruit. "I made this salad with fruits from the arboretum," he said. "No two of them come from the same world. If you'd like, I can tell you the history of each one of them."

Prilla wasn't so sure about listening to a lecture on the xeno-biology of fruit, but the salad looked extremely tasty. Prilla stepped aside, long enough for Antari to float his way in.

Next, Aniel explained that while she had no interest in trying the crepelettes, as her mechanical body would be unable to process them, she had heard so much about them, she had prepared a poem in their honor. She hoped to join the festivities and recite her poem for them. Prilla didn't know what to think of that. It made her feel all fluttery under her feathers. So, she waved Aniel on in.

Finally, Ryeh stepped forward and gave her ruffle-feathered friend a hug. "I could tell you were feeling lonely last night," Ryeh said. "So, I thought you'd like it if I brought some of your friends over to share your crepelette feast with you. I hope you don't mind."

Prilla was still confused about her feelings, but she was glad that she wouldn't have to eat her feast alone. "No," Prilla said to her friend, "I don't mind."

The friends sat down to a feast of grassberry crepelettes, foreign fruits, and Almachian wine. It was a blissful combination of the familiar, the novel, and the extravagant for Prilla.

As the others ate, Aniel recited her poem and then expounded on poetic theory—a subject she had been studying in an advanced class she took during her lunches. After the meal, Antari dropped heavily onto his chair, his swimbladder barely able to counteract the weight of all the good food. He proceeded to tell the history and ecology of each of the fruits they'd eaten, just as he'd promised. The evening ended with Yss recounting the clever haggling she'd done to acquire the Almachian wine. By the end of her story—which involved a fixed poker game, a race around the nearest ringed planet, and more flirting than one would expect from a cold-blooded alien —the rest of them were looking ready to depart.

Prilla enjoyed the windows into her friends' lives that their conversations provided, but she realized that she would no more want to help Yss haggle with an Almach wine baron, practice xeno-ecology with Antari, or study poetic theory with Aniel than they had wanted to help her grow grassberries. The many components of the evening's feast had been acquired separately, but they were enjoyed together. And that was what mattered.

2

———

WINGED FOLK ONLY

"You can't come on the voyage," the Ululu sneered, folding his wings in a very cross manner. "Winged folk only."

Evben tried to object, but all the other avians lounging about the bar took up the Ululu's catchy cry: "That's right! Winged folk only!" The feathers around the Ululu's eyes crinkled happily; if he hadn't been a beaked species, he'd have been grinning. The Ululu had been looking for a way to exclude Evben from Avian Night at the All Alien Cafe since she'd first started coming, but the cafe owner stood up for the little mousey alien's right to participate. Even if she wasn't any sort of bird.

"Fine," Evben squeaked at the much larger aliens. "I'll get wings." She jumped off the gigantic bar stool and did her best tiny impression of storming out while the cackling avian laughter echoed in her big round ears.

There were five weeks until the avian voyage to New Jupiter, the closest gas giant to Crossroads Station. That wasn't enough time for Evben to teach herself engineering and design her own wings, but she had some savings, and a robot friend who worked at Robots 4 Robots was able to get her a rush order on a special commission. Robots 4 Robots didn't usually take commissions for organic augmentations, but they'd built winged robots before, so they had the necessary designs. Besides, a pair of wings small enough for Evben—her species was among the tiniest aliens on Crossroads Station—required so little ultra-light aluminum that the cost of the materials was next to nothing.

When the avians lined up for the shuttle to New Jupiter with their space helmets under their wings, Evban cautiously joined the end of the line. She held her own tiny space helmet with one paw, and she twisted the tip of her long tail nervously with the other. One by one, the avians boarded the shuttle, but when Evban tried to get onboard, the Ululu blocked her path with one of his long stick-like legs.

"No wings, no ride," he said.

Evban put down her space helmet, tucked her paws into the handholds on the metal wings folded tight against her back, and then she spread her arms—the metal blades of the mechanical wings fanned out. They felt so good on Evban's back, sprouting from her shoulder blades like real wings should, that she skipped a little dance and twirled. Her long tail followed her, and her wings fanned gracefully.

The Ululu snorted. "Those aren't real wings," he said, but one of the other avian aliens—a double-winged Eechie—saw Evban's little dance and screeched excitedly.

"I already have two sets of wings, but those are so cute, maybe I should get another one!"

Several puff-feathered Rennten peeked out to see what all the commotion was about and immediately began cooing over Evban and her tiny metal wings. It was more attention than any of the avians—other than the Ululu—had ever paid to Evban before.

The Ululu's feathers ruffled angrily, but he had been overruled. Evban scurried between his long legs and boarded the space shuttle with the others.

On the flight to New Jupiter, the Rennten clucked traditional roosting songs, and the Eechie did a double-winged dance that had them all flapping in laughter. Evban flapped her little metal wings right along with them. She'd never been happier.

New Jupiter swelled in the space shuttle's windows like a red and gold balloon. When it filled the entire horizon, the s'rellick shuttle captain turned to her avian passengers and hissed with her forked tongue, "Helmetssss on!"

Amidst much clucking and cawing, all the avians put on their helmets. They looked like they'd stuck their heads in bubbles.

"We're sssskimming the atmosssphere," the s'rellick captain hissed. "When I pop the hatch, go have your fun. I'll sssswing by to pick everyone up in a few hourssss."

The Renntens hopped about giddily, and the Eechie stretched her wings, readying to fly. The Ululu glared at Evban over his beak and said, "There's no shame in staying on the shuttle."

When the hatch popped, Evban was the first to run, jump, and flap her way into the thin New Jupiter atmosphere. Pink and gold clouds streamed past her, dispersing in the wind of her wings. She was free! She was one of the avians! She was... falling.

Evban tumbled through the golden clouds; their colors thickened and deepened through shades of orange to brown. Evban flapped her ultra-light aluminum wings as hard as her little arms could, but she didn't have the strength for it. She kept falling.

Until thump, she landed on the feathered back of the Ululu. "You're not a bird," he said, and in spite of her wings, Evban found herself in no position to argue with him. She readied herself for his rebuke. "But you have wings, and you should learn to use them better than that. Don't flap. Glide."

The Ululu shook Evban off his back, and the little mousie creature found herself falling through New Jupiter's clouds again. But she focused on the Ululu's words and tilted her wings this time. Instead of pushing with all her strength, she leaned into the gas giant's winds.

"There you go," the Ululu said. "Now you're flying."

Evban lowered one wing and spiraled around, feeling the rush that she'd heard the avians talk about.

"Keep close," the Ululu said. "I didn't sign up for giving flying lessons, but I don't want to see you fall into the crushing depths of a gas giant either."

Evban circled back with her long tail streaming out behind her. She settled into the Ululu's backdraft and squeaked quietly, "Thank you."

The Ululu grumbled, "Don't mention it," but he didn't fly away. After the two of them soared in formation for a few minutes, the Ululu added, "You're not used to flying, so your wings may get tired. If you need to, you can rest on my back again." Evban heard a touch of respect in his voice.

3

GO HIGH

EVBAN FLAPPED her mechanical wings joyously, dipping and swooping through New Jupiter's soupy pink-and-gold clouds. Her whiskers tickled against the glassy bubble of her breathing-helmet, and her long tail streamed out behind her. She'd drifted away from the flock of avian aliens. Their organic wings were broader and stronger than her little mechanical ones, but she knew her friends would come back for her before the space shuttle returned for them all.

Evban spiraled downward, toward the crushing heart of the gas giant. The clouds changed shape as she flew; wispy yellow cirrus clouds gave way to puffy auburn cumulus. In the distance beneath her, a purple nimbus cloud loomed, flashing with jagged lines of lightning.

Her avian friends wouldn't be safe in a cloud like that, but Evban's mechanical wings were coated with electrical dampeners that would shield her from the lightning. Perhaps while her friends, with their strong organic wings, were flying fast and far in the upper clouds, Evban could have an adventure to tell them about in that amethyst storm cloud. She folded her wings in close and dove.

Maybe it was in her mind, but Evban felt her fur prickle with electricity as soon as the purple cloud closed around her. It was dark, and her eyes took a moment to adjust while she winged blind. Then shapes appeared in the darkness; frilly finned fish-like shapes, swimming through the cloud she was flying through.

Cautiously, Evban edged towards one of the fish-shapes. It was many times larger than even the largest of her avian friends, and when she got close enough, Evban could see that its skin was amorphous or translucent. She could see through the edges of it, almost as if her eyes were playing tricks on her in the dark. Were her eyes playing tricks on her?

Lightning flashed, and the purple billows of the cloud glowed. In the momentary light, the fish-shape crystallized, and Evban saw herself reflected in its large eyes. Its wide round mouth moved, swallowing or speaking—Evban wasn't sure, but she imagined a voice in her head saying, "Go high," except that it was more of a concept than actual words.

Before Evban could decide whether to heed the gas giant alien's advice, lightning flashed again. This time, Evban saw herself reflected in its large eye without her helmet or wings on: simply a small mousy alien, floating alone in the clouds of New Jupiter. Another flash, and her reflection was no longer alone: she was surrounded by her large litter of siblings, back in their burrow on her homeworld. She was shocked by the detail of the image—each one of her dozens of siblings, actually as they would be now, years older than when she'd last seen them.

The flashes of lightning came faster and brighter, each one pulling her deeper into a story unfolding in the fish alien's eye. She aged, she danced, she played, she mated and raised her own litter of mousie kittens—all in the fish's eye—and each of her children aged, danced, played, mated and raised their own litters of mousie kittens, again and again, generations of her family growing and dying in the eyes of an alien fish.

Evban grew so mesmerized by the vision, she forgot to flap her wings and began falling deeper into New Jupiter's dark purple clouds. The fish followed her, watching her closely, mirroring her fractally expanding lives in its unblinking eye. Finally, centuries since she'd heard them before, the fish's words echoed in her mind again, "Go high!"

This time, Evban shook herself through the eons and flapped her mechanical wings as hard as her little arms could. The fish's mouth opened beneath her as she rose higher and higher through the cloud. All of her lifetimes fell away, and Evban became convinced the gas giant fish would eat her. Her entire existence reduced to a single chase scene: could she outfly the alien fish?

When Evban burst free of the nimbus cloud, her head began to clear. She checked the readings on her wrist-monitor: the gases in the purple cloud had psycho-active elements in them. Had the fish known? Had there been a fish at all?

Evban saw the flock of her friends in the distance, helmet bubbles around their heads and broad wings flapping strongly toward her. She had wanted to regale them with her adventures, but when she thought about the secret lifetimes she'd lived on her homeworld inside the fish's eye, she decided to keep them to herself.

"How's our little mousie?" the closest bird, a long-legged crane-like Ululu cawed. "You haven't been swallowed whole by the clouds of New Jupiter?"

Evban thought of the fish and said, "Or maybe I have been, but I came out alive."

4

I AM MAZILLION

ONE OF MY scouts flies through the space station's ductwork. Another flies out among the aliens who are crowding through the dock and maneuvers above them, looking down, seeing where I am, what this space station is like. Most of me clusters in a high corner out of sight, near the airlock I've painstakingly flown through, one body at a time, unnoticed, tiny, unimportant. The spaceship I arrived on doesn't know it had a stowaway, let alone a thousand, bound together telepathically. A thousand tiny bodies, each many-legged with shimmering pairs of wings. One mind. I am Mazillion, and I am the first of my species in space.

An alien vessel piloted by bipedal mammals came to my planet, and I snuck aboard. I didn't want the mammals to know about me, so I kept my bodies huddled close, balled up together, wings held still, no buzzing. I listened to the mammals moan and gibber. Eventually, I realized their vocalizations were a form of speech. Slabs of meat in their mouths danced, and they listened to the ripples and waves in the air made by the dancing. It seemed a strange way to talk: so much easier to watch a dance than to reverse-engineer it from the wake it leaves in the air.

Occasionally, I sent feelers out—single scouts, bodies with only six legs and one pair of wings apiece—to search for food. But I found no scraps of food left out by the mammals, and I didn't dare risk discovery. Instead, I cannibalized myself— eight-legged bodies eating six-legged bodies; ten-legged bodies eating eight-legged bodies, saving as much of my own complexity as I could.

A tenth of my bodies died on that trip through deep, cold space. Decimated.

I wondered so many times if it was worth it.

Would I die, having seen nothing more than the stars from a new angle to show for my bravery? True—the ascent from my homeworld had been stunning. My people have theorized for many lifetimes that our world is a sphere. I am the only one who has seen it. But my voyage turned out to be a one way trip, and now I am stranded on this space station.

My scout from the empty ducts returns. My scout from the crowded docks flies almost beyond the reach of my telepathic neural network. I feel dizzy, flying over all these bizarre aliens. I almost forget myself, consumed by wanting to see just one more bizarre sight: flower-covered plants that stroll and roll like tumbleweeds; smooth-skinned, glistening amphibians with powerful hind legs and bulging eyes; and so many fur-covered mammal species. All of them seemingly sentient. The least of them is more advanced than the most brilliant minds on my world... because they are here. In space. And only I, from my own species, have made it this far. And even I, only by hitchhik- ing. Who would have thought mammals and frogs would be so successful? The plants do not surprise me. I have always admired plants for their patience and tranquility.

I summon self control and pull myself back together, bringing my scout body back to myself. All my bodies dance and buzz and whir with excitement, twitching legs, flittering wings. I am of two minds, and I cannot resolve the internal conflict. Part of me wants to hide in the ductwork, grow stronger, sneaking out only when necessary to seek out food and sustenance.

Another part though—strong and brave—wants to do something new. Something we have never done before. Become something new.

I consider my options, laying low to begin with. But as the weeks pass, the adventurous part of me grows stronger. More and more of my bodies agree. To live among these one-bodied aliens, I must become like them. At least, a little. I will engage in mimicry, an age-old tradition among successful insect species. So many of our ancestors developed bodies that physically mimicked the shapes of plants for disguise or the shapes of predatory avians for protection. Together, my selves will come into a single shape and mimic a new type of body, for a new reason.

When I have come to a decision, all of my bodies in harmonious dancing agreement, then I descend, one body at a time, pouring down from the ductwork into a dense shape. My bodies pack close together, wings and legs brushing against each other. Some of my bodies become feet, hovering slightly above the space station's metal floor. Rising from the feet, my bodies form two columns, combining into a trunk and then splitting apart again—two arms with a head in-between.

I stand in the quiet corridor that my scout bodies selected. My densely packed bodies rise together on one side, lifting our left arm. I have seen how the bipedal aliens walk, lifting one leg after the other. That is too hard for my thousand-fold bodies. Together, my selves float forward, straining to hold our shape. In this way, I float into the crowds of bipedal aliens whom I've only ever watched from above before.

The aliens step aside, giving me space. A red-furred canine

tilts its head, inquisitively. A green-skinned amphibian makes a gulping noise, reminding me uncomfortably of sub-sentient amphibious predators from my homeworld. My bodies are frightened and lose their cohesion; momentarily, my new bipedal forms flies apart into an amorphous cloud. But I exert great will-power; the dancing of all of my bodies harmonizes, and I pull myself back together.

A biped. Like all the other bipeds. Floating through the crowded station halls. Okay, not exactly like all the other bipeds. But close enough.

I float towards a place that my scouts have seen—a place called The All Alien Cafe. I have seen through my scouts' multi-faceted eyes that all kinds of aliens congregate here. I enter, approach the bar, and with some difficulty, send a dance rippling among my closely-packed bodies telling them to hold their form, but bend in the middle. I simulate sitting on a barstool, floating above it actually.

A feeling of pride fills the thorax of every one of my bodies. The bartender approaches me. The bipedal bartender has a long, prehensile nose and asks with those strange moaning sounds, "What can I get you?"

My scouts have seen this, watching other aliens at this bar. I have learned the language that most of the aliens speak here by listening closely. I know what to say, and my bodies shudder their wings together, buzzing in a carefully modulated way: "ONE SUGAR JUICE PLEAZZZZE."

The elephantine bartender nods and says, "Coming right up." Moments later, the bartender places a frosted glass filled with a pink liquid in front of me.

"THANKZZZZ," I buzz with all of the wings of all of my bodies in concert. Then I enjoy the cold, sweet beverage, letting each of my bodies take a turn perching on the glass lip of the cup and dipping their own tiny proboscises into the sticky, sugary pink juice.

I have succeeded, and it tastes sweet. I am a biped now. At least, when I want to be.

5

———

HIDDEN FEELINGS

THE SPINES on S'lisha's neck twitched, but she kept them from extending into a thorny display of her anger. The spaceship captain wanted the boxes of robot arms on his cargo deck rearranged yet again. If he'd explained himself clearly in the first place, it would have saved so much time. S'lisha seethed silently and imagined crushing the spaceship captain with his own cargo.

"Wow, the captain sure got on your nerves," Malcolm said. "You looked like you wanted to tear his head off."

S'lisha had been working with Malcolm for several months on this ship, and the small human had an uncanny knack for sensing her emotions. However, she'd researched it, and humans weren't actually telepathic. He was only guessing. He could prove nothing.

"Are you afraid of me?" S'lisha said. Usually, she clammed up when Malcolm called her on her emotions, afraid of playing into the violent stereotype of her species. She'd been told that they looked like miniature dragons to humans, whatever that meant.

"No." Malcolm affixed an anti-grav unit to one of the cargo

crates and lifted it up to stack it the way the captain wanted. "Where did you get that idea?"

S'lisha lifted one of the crates herself. She didn't need an anti-grav unit. "You're always telling me about these violent images you have of me. Snapping necks. Breaking arms." She didn't stop her voice from hissing in the way humans found so disconcerting. "You should look into that. Being plagued by violent imagery can be a sign of depression in your species."

At the word depression, a small round medi-bot came flying over. Blue and green lights twinkled on the medi-bot as it spoke: "Depression is a very serious issue on a spaceship."

"I'm not depressed." Malcolm glared at S'lisha.

"You are plagued by violent images?" Blue and yellow twinkly light this time. Apparently, the medi-bot had heard more than the word 'depression.'

"He told me that he was picturing the captain being decapitated," S'lisha offered helpfully.

Red and yellow twinkly lights: "Please accompany me to the medical bay."

Malcolm grumbled, but he followed the medi-bot docilely out of the cargo bay. As S'lisha watched him go, she relished imagining her scaled talons shredding the small human's arms and legs.

But she knew better than to say anything about it.

6

HIDDEN INTENTIONS

"Can you breathe fire if you eat rocket fuel?" asked Alison, the captain's five-year-old daughter.

S'lisha drew a deep, calming breath through her scaly nostrils. She didn't understand why humans brought their children on spaceships. Her species kept their larval offspring in caves on their home world until they matured and their adult scales grew in. They didn't feel an obsessive need to keep the grubs nearby. Or to pawn them off on lower officers for "babysitting."

"*Can you?*" Alison demanded.

"No," S'lisha grumbled, watching the pink-skinned primate grapple with the controls for the hatchway into the shuttlecraft's small engine room—where the child probably imagined the "rocket fuel" was stored. Fortunately, the controls could be locked from the shuttlecraft's main dash. "I told you, I'm not a dragon."

"You're a boring old alien." Frustrated, the child started kicking the hatch door.

"Stop that!" S'lisha roared, her reptilian voice like metal scraping against stone.

The human child stopped kicking the hatch door and stared at her. She tilted her small oval face to the side. "Can you breathe fire if you get angry enough?"

S'lisha wanted to claw the child's little face off, but the captain wouldn't like that. And she needed this job. She just needed to put up with the child for another hour while she finished cataloging the asteroids here for mineral deposits worth mining. Then she could fly the shuttlecraft back to the main ship and dump the human larva back into the hands of her usual caretakers.

Children didn't need "field trips." They needed quiet caves to mature in.

"Here—" S'lisha shoved the knapsack the child had come with towards her. "Use your art supplies. Draw an asteroid."

"They're boooring gray."

Cataloging asteroids could be soothing work—her only break from working with mammals day in and day out. It wasn't with Alison along. "*Paint them whatever color you want.*"

Alison brightened at that suggestion, and S'lisha had time to run several more scans before she realized Alison wasn't coloring in drawings of asteroids on her art tablet—she'd begun painting on the side viewscreen.

S'lisha roared, much like Alison imagined an angry dragon would roar. Alison clapped and cried, "Now breathe fire!"

S'lisha could not win with this child. She needed a way to contain her grabby little arms and kicky little feet. There weren't a lot of options in a Class Z shuttlecraft. Looking the shuttle over, S'lisha's slitted eyes landed on the airlock.

"Have you ever played spacers and dragons?" S'lisha hissed the words—soft and deadly like silk tearing on a knife.

Alison put down her paintbrush, dripping yellow blobs on the shuttle's floor. "No... How do you play?" She sounded excited, hopeful.

Good.

"First, put on your spacesuit."

S'lisha had to help Alison get her arms and legs into her custom child-sized spacesuit. Once it was safely sealed—child-locked so that Alison couldn't accidentally depressurize it—S'lisha said, "Next, you hide in the airlock."

"Hide from what?" Alison's voice, broadcast from her helmet, crackled over the ship's speakers.

S'lisha raised her scaly arms and spread her vestigial wings in a way that she thought Alison would find appropriately frightening and said, "The scary DRAGON!"

Alison doubled over laughing, the sound tinny and staticky over the ship's speakers. Finally, she pulled herself together and said, "Okay!"

She climbed into the airlock all on her own. The smooth walls of the airlock cradled her like a larva cave. She didn't balk at all when S'lisha sealed it around her or cycled the atmosphere out.

She did start to scream when the outer door opened and the shuttlecraft began to accelerate away from her. S'lisha assured her over the radio, "There's nothing to fear. I'll be back for you in an hour or so. And you're very well hidden from any *dragons*."

S'lisha turned down the sound of the speakers as she piloted the shuttlecraft away from the furious but safely contained child, floating among the asteroids.

7

GREEN SKIN DEEP

"We're so much alike," Trinth said, forming the sound of the words through her flute-like reeds. She certainly didn't look much like S'lisha, a reptilian alien. Trinth looked more like a cosmic rosebush—she saw through flower-like eyes; spoke with flute-like reeds; and used grasping vines to walk and grab.

S'lisha supposed that Trinth's leaves were mostly green, as were S'lisha's scales. They had that in common. They were both green.

Trinth unfurled the leaves around her pink-petaled flower eyes. "The humans don't understand us," she said. "We have to stick together."

"That's true," S'lisha agreed, looking around the spaceship cafeteria. Humans *did not* understand her. In fact, Trinth was the first member of the crew who had ever joined S'lisha at her table during a meal. The humans either ignored her, called her a "dragon," or made jokes about whether her food was "fresh enough." *Because eating dead food is soooo much more appetizing.* Trinth didn't even eat, and yet, here she was. It gave S'lisha a warm feeling in her cold-blooded belly to think that maybe this beautiful angiosperm alien understood. "At least the humans pay well."

"They do..." Trinth's vines twisted and twined together. "But they keep it so hot." She held forth some of her leaves, browned at the edges. "I'm wilting."

S'lisha raged inside. *How could the humans do this to such a delicate creature?* Sure, S'lisha actually found the spaceship a little too cold, but she was tough and could take it. The humans would be okay a few degrees colder; they had coats they could wear. What was Trinth supposed to do? Poor wilting thing. "I'll take care of it," S'lisha said.

On the way to her next shift in the cargo bay, S'lisha ducked into engineering and furtively turned the ship's thermostat down several degrees. The humans shivered for half a day before they figured it out and turned the temperature back up. But Trinth's leaves looked greener and brighter for the few hours of relief. So S'lisha made a habit of turning the temperature down whenever she could. No one would ever suspect her since S'rellicks came from a much hotter planet, and it *couldn't* be Trinth as she never went anywhere near engineering.

Over the next several weeks, Trinth made a habit of stopping by S'lisha's otherwise empty table during lunch.

Trinth mentioned how hard it was to come by ionizing radiation on the spaceship, so the next time a shipment of ion bulbs came through the cargo bay, S'lisha nabbed a few extra ones for her new friend to use in her quarters. Trinth mentioned how tiresome it was to always speak in a language designed for metazoan mouths, so S'lisha downloaded a primer for learning Trinth's language. Trinth complained that the water rations were never enough for her, so S'lisha offered to donate some of hers. She was from a desert world; she didn't need so much water.

It was nice to finally have a friend.

When the ship docked at Crossroads Station to refuel and

pick up cargo, one of the new shipments was signed for by a photosynthoid alien like Trinth, only this one had darker leaves and blue eye-flowers. S'lisha was about to show off her new linguistic abilities, which she'd been too self-conscious to test on Trinth, when Trinth rustled into the cargo bay.

The two photosynthoid aliens greeted each other in their own language, sounding like a dance of bells and wind chimes.

"That's beautiful," one of the human cargo haulers murmured. "Are they singing?"

S'lisha felt extremely clever and superior for actually understanding that Trinth had said, "*It's been so long!*" and the newcomer had replied, "*I didn't know you worked here!*" A moment more, and S'lisha would have shown off by translating. However, the tintinnabulous conversation continued too quickly.

"*I've been so terribly lonely!*" Trinth chimed. "*Everyone here is awful!*"

The newcomer's blue flower-eyes turned toward S'lisha. "*Humans are bad enough. You're working on a ship with a s'rellick?*"

Trinth's leaves wrung, and she said in a voice like a waterfall of bells, "*At least the lizard is stupid. I have her tricked into giving me half her water ration—*"

S'lisha's scales spiked up, and she stomped out of the cargo bay, needing to hear no more from a weakling plant. She'd been a fool to value the plant's friendship. Their similarity had only ever run skin deep.

On her way past engineering, S'lisha turned up the temperature and broke the thermostat. Warm air flooded out of the spaceship's heating vents. It would take the humans at least a week to fix it.

8

MANY TINY FEET

S'LISHA TRACED her scaly claw over the transparent metal surface of the incubator. It was the most complex cargo crate that she'd ever seen—heating and cooling coils all around the sides, a humidifier built into the base, and brackets inside to hold all of the eggs carefully in place. It had come with detailed instructions for all the settings—cool at first, but warmer and moister over time.

The eggs inside were translucent, oval, and all lined up in rows. S'lisha could make out the dancing shadows of fetal creatures, angular and leggy, moving inside their membranous shells. S'lisha found their movements mesmerizing and had taken a moment to stop and watch them every day since the crate had arrived onboard.

She could swear that today the baby arachnids—or whatever they were—moved more slowly. She tapped her claws against the side of the crate, hoping to rouse them.

"Don't fiddle with that!" Greecha shouted. She glided across the cargo bay on her mechanical treads. "If the settings on this crate vary at all from the specifications, our buyer doesn't have to pay." Greecha was a robo-lifeform. She followed and enforced rules exactly as written, making her an extraordinarily reliable employee, but also an inflexible one.

S'lisha tried reasoning with Greecha anyway: "They're dying."

"Not our problem."

Predictable. S'lisha snorted.

As soon as Greecha left the cargo bay, S'lisha experimented with the temperature and moisture settings on the incubator until the fetal shadows began moving again as they had before. *Lively, lithe shadows.* The sight of their dancing made the tip of S'lisha's spiked tail curl with pleasure.

But she couldn't allow Greecha to discover what she'd done. So S'lisha checked the corridor, saw it was clear, and surreptitiously wheeled the incubator to her own quarters. Once the incubator was safely hidden under her bed, S'lisha locked her quarters and made her way to the bridge. Cargo-workers didn't usually visit the bridge, so the captain—a human female—wasn't pleased to see the reptilian alien.

"What do you want?" Captain Corridan frowned her pink primate lips.

"There's some rotting cargo stinking up the cargo bay," S'lisha said, lying with her forked tongue. "Whaddaya want me to do with it?"

Captain Corridan's hands were full with data-pads of star maps. She didn't even look at S'lisha as she said, "*Deal* with it. That's your job."

"Space it?" S'lisha asked.

One of the pilots, another human, came over to the captain to confer about possible course adjustments. The captain was too busy to remember a cargo-worker asking to be micromanaged. That was fine by S'lisha. She had what she needed.

NEXT SHIFT, Greecha accused S'lisha of messing with the incubator, and S'lisha said matter-of-factly, "It was rotting. Captain said to space it."

Greecha grumbled, the gears in her voice box grinding, but she couldn't countermand the captain. "You could have emptied and cleaned it."

S'lisha shuddered, the scales along her back rippling at the idea of cleaning out an incubator filled with rotten eggs. "No *thanks*," she hissed.

Greecha's mechanical eyes telescoped outward to stare at S'lisha pointedly. "If we get charged for it, it's coming out of *your* paycheck."

S'lisha wasn't worried. She'd probably get a medal for saving the baby arachnids when they arrived at their destination still alive due exclusively to S'lisha's heroics. Maybe Greecha would be punished by being torn apart and sold as scrap metal.

In the mean time, Greecha punished S'lisha by making her rearrange the heaviest cargo—for safety reasons, of course— and then changing her mind and making S'lisha put it all back. *As if Greecha was actually changing her mind.* With that mechanical brain, she had the optimal safety pattern mapped out for any configuration of cargo instantly. S'lisha hated robots.

By the end of her shift, S'lisha stumbled into her quarters, ready to hibernate for a hundred years. Or else murder a hundred stupid robots.

She was greeted by the sight of gossamer rainbows on shining lines of silken thread, widely spaced throughout most of the room but densely woven around her bed where the incubator was hidden.

S'isha navigated the room, nimbly careful to avoid the lines of silk. She didn't want to break them. At the edge of her bed she crouched, statue still, until the tiny arachnids dared to show themselves. Their faceted eyes glittered like diamonds; their tiny carapaces shone like mother-of-pearl; and their delicate legs pulled at the strands of silk, as if they were still deciding what to do—whether to explore the reptilian biped that had entered their realm or hide from her in fear.

S'lisha sang to the arachnids in the guttural, bellowing tones of her native language—a sound that the humans onboard had compared to a giant frog dying. The baby arachnids, however, seemed to like it and swung on gossamer threads to her. They landed lightly on her scaled shoulders and head spikes. With busy legs, they wove a shawl of silk that settled over S'lisha like the peace she'd known as a mere hatchling in the hibernation caves on her homeworld.

For weeks, S'lisha sang to the baby arachnids at night and slept under their soft silk, saddened when she had to leave them in the morning for her shifts. She cared for them, feeding them from her own rations until the ship docked at a waystation, and she was able to surreptitiously buy a supply of feeder flies from an avian merchant.

The baby arachnids greeted S'lisha at the end of her shifts by swinging eagerly across the room to rest on her arms and shoulders. They danced when she sang, tickling the soft spaces between her scales with their tiny feet. They skittered around the room, playing and chasing each other, wrestling until S'lisha laughed at their antics.

Humans had compared S'lisha's laugh to a komodo dragon hiccupping. That was fine. She didn't care what the humans thought, and besides, they rarely gave her anything worth laughing at.

The arachnids, however, *laughed with her*, delighted by the sound of her laughter. At least, that's what S'lisha thought it meant when they clapped their little feet together.

They made her so happy.

ON THE DAY that the incubator's buyer was scheduled to come for his shipment, S'lisha prowled nervously through the cargo bay. She skulked past the crates of his cargo, wishing her scales were chromataphylic like some members of her species. Then she could disappear, camouflaged, while she waited for him, rather than ducking guiltily away every time Greecha glared at her with those telescopic eyes.

When the cargo bay door lifted, a mammalian alien with broad, hunched, furry shoulders lumbered in. He was a Torofor —not at all what S'lisha had expected. Fuzzy mammaloids rarely kept insectoids of any type as pets, let alone arachnids. The mammaloid fear of leggy exoskeletons was strangely universal.

Greecha wheeled her way across the cargo bay to meet the Torofor, and then led him toward his pile of crates. As he passed a pair of human cargo workers, one of them whispered to the other, *"That's one big bear,"* reducing yet another sentient species to a shadow of some pre-sentient animal from the human's homeworld.

The Torofor examined the pile of crates before huffing an accusation: "I don't see the incubator. It's delicate. How dare you have crushed it under all these hardier crates!"

The lenses in Greecha's telescope eyes flashed red as she said, "One of our cargo workers threw that one out. Apparently, it was rotting."

S'lisha was about to step forward, defend her honor, and declaim the safety of the Torofor's precious arachnids to him, when he growled, "They're *supposed* to rot. That's the whole point of the incubator—fermented Salisal eggs are a *delicacy*."

In honesty, S'lisha couldn't feel horrified. Fermented arachnid eggs did sound delicious. She certainly ate her fair share of insects.

However, she also didn't feel the need to tell an angry Torofor what had really happened to his expensive delicacy.

Let Greecha dock her pay.

S'lisha slipped silently out of the cargo bay and returned to her quarters, where she was greeted by silken rainbows, sparkly multi-faceted eyes, and the embrace of many tiny feet.

9

____

WHERE THE HEART IS

ANY HUMAN in the room would have seen an oversized koala bear, a bushy red-wolf, a long-tailed, green lizard, and a large blue fish wearing a diving helmet, floating bizarrely above his barstool. But there were no humans in the room. It was the *All Alien Cafe* on the interstellar meeting point known as Crossroads Station.

"Do you ever miss your home worlds?" the red-wolf asked the others. He was a Heffen, and his species were refugees from a planet whose yellow dwarf star had expanded into a red giant. "I miss the wide open savannahs," he said, ears pointed forward and his long, canid nose pointed down.

The other three exchanged worried looks. They could tell when their friend was feeling melancholy. Over the years, the four of them had learned to read each other quite well, despite their very different physiologies. The koala, in particular, was tuned into every nuance of the Heffen's mood, and the expression in her sparkling eyes became especially concerned.

"Are you kidding?" the fish said, followed by a burp of heavy gases from the shimmery blue gills along his sleek body. His swim-bladder lightened thusly, the Lintar bobbed inches upward in the air. "My home world is the only place I can't fly." He swirled his long, silky fins gracefully.

Lintars evolved on a planet with a much thinner atmosphere than filled the metal bulk of Crossroads Station. As a tradeoff, they had to wear breathing helmets with air filters and other complex breathing apparatuses on Crossroads Station—and in other nitrogen rich atmospheres—but they could fly.

The Srellik flicked her forked tongue in a dismissive hiss. Her scaly, green hide sparkled in the bar's low light. "Dirtballs are for pre-tech savages," she said.

The Heffen continued staring bleakly into the drink clutched tightly between his paws. His friends' levity wasn't helping.

"Isn't this why we don't talk about home worlds?" the Woaoo said, with a quaver in her voice. Her face was flat with a large, oval nose, and her gray fur was short, except where it lengthened into two silver clouds around her ears. "It's depressing," she said. "You'll only upset yourself."

Every time the Heffen started talking like this, the Woaoo found her mind plagued by a sequence of paintings she'd had the misfortune to imagine. They flitted through her mind, depicting the Heffen—his handsome face grown gaunt and his ruddy fur thinning—as he descended deeper and deeper into depression, drugs, and eventually suicide. She would never paint such images for fear that they would prove prophetic. Yet, the vision haunted her. She couldn't stand the idea of her life without him.

She placed a comforting paw on the Heffen's broad shoulder, hoping to reassure herself as much as him, but he pulled abruptly away.

"Denial," he said. "That's what it is. Aren't you sick of it?"

The Srellik and Lintar exchanged a glance that communicated their amused disdain for over-emotional warmbloods, but neither said anything.

"My home world is a burnt up ball of charred coal now!" the Heffen barked. "I used to lie out in the long savannah grass with the cool breeze in my fur..." His eyes went soft, and his wolfish face grew rapturous at the memory. The expression only lasted a moment, and then he hardened into the Heffen they all knew. "And then some godforsaken government scientist with his crazy engineering schemes got his calculations wrong... and I live here. In a metal box, orbiting a foreign star."

They'd all heard this story before. The Heffen sun would have died slowly over thousands of years... but an attempt to kick-start the fading yellow dwarf left the Heffen people refugees from the blasting heat of a red giant in a mere decade. It pulled at the Woaoo's heart strings every time. Her poor Heffen. Too lost in the pain of the past to notice her affection... "Does it help to talk?" she asked, trying to keep her voice from shaking.

"Maybe," he said. He turned his soulful, troubled eyes up from the drink he was nursing and gave the Woao a look that stopped her heart. "Why don't you ever go home?" he asked her. "I know you miss it."

The Woaoo laughed, a tinkling, chittery sound filled with worry, sore nerves, and giddiness. "I can't afford the fare." She laughed, but her expression was serious. Her dark eyes were locked onto the Heffen's, greedy for every moment of his soulful gaze. "Besides, it's not as if I have anyone to visit there. Not like my friends here."

The Heffen snorted, and the moment ended. He dipped his muzzle back toward his drink. Her story was as familiar to them all as his.

The Woaoo had been outcast from her society for composing heretical artwork. Everyone she had thought she loved had turned on her. It was a past that her friends on Crossroads Station had trouble reconciling with the cheerful, adorable Woaoo they knew. She did not seem like a dangerous heretic. Nonetheless, they were impressed by her story and often asked to see some of her heretical artwork. She would only show them the ergonomically pleasing exo-skeletal cases that she designed for a robotic pet company these days.

"You miss the *place* though, don't you?" the Heffen asked.

The Woaoo nodded. She missed the planet she'd been born on more than words could say, but it was not an all consuming passion. It was nothing compared to the loss the Heffen had suffered. Nor the loss she feared she would suffer if she ever lost him.

"Tell you what," the Heffen said, looking down at his companion. "Let's save up. We can all go in together and buy a spaceship..." he looked at the Srellik and Lintar, "...get out of this tin can whenever we want."

"I have a spaceship," the Srellik said.

All three of the others looked at her. Brown Heffen eyes, darker Woaoo eyes, and wide, limpid Lintar eyes obscured by the shielding of his breathing helmet stared at the Srellik. They all knew she was a cargo-hauler, but they'd never heard of her using her spaceship for recreation. Ever. Naturally, they'd assumed it wasn't actually hers. Only leased.

"Wonderful!" the Lintar said, clapping his fins. The delicate appendages made only the lightest feathery sound. Then, he turned a little pirouette, floating in the air above his barstool. His draping fins twirled out like the skirt of a ball gown. "Let's all go on a trip!"

The Woaoo clasped her heavily clawed paws together, and the Heffen's ears perked up. Hope was in both their eyes.

"Look what you've done," the Srellk hissed. Her lidless eyes glittered angrily as she stared at the Lintar. "You've gotten the warmbloods' hopes up."

"Me?" said the Lintar, his thick lipped mouth forming an *O*.

"You're the one who mentioned having a ship. I don't think you would have if you didn't secretly want to use it."

"I use it!" the Srellik hissed. "I carry freight from here to the mining asteroids and back again, three times daily."

"Sounds thrilling," the Lintar said, rolling his eyes inside his breathing helm. "Perhaps you need a vacation?" The Lintar held the Srellik's lidless gaze while decadently sucking his drink noisily up through a straw fitted to a slot in his breathing helmet.

The Woaoo coughed lightly to get her companions' attention. "When I was a joey," she said, "my family would go camping in the forests outside Tway-wa-a City." Her smooth gray fur ruffled and twitched as she spoke, a tic that generally connoted great emotion in her. She couldn't give the Heffen his world back, but maybe it would help him to share her world. And maybe it would help him to understand her.

"I would sit by our campfire at night," she said, "surrounded by whistling trees and twiney vines, and look up at the stars. All I could think was how much I wanted to be up there, among the stars. Now all I can think..." she said, sitting on a space station, orbiting a cold foreign star, "...is how how much I wish I could go back there again." The words weren't true. The wish dearest to the Woao's heart sat right in front of her with flowing red fur and brooding eyes. But, she knew her audience, and her words were gauged to affect the Srellik.

The Srellik glared at her. Even with lidless reptilian eyes, the coldblooded Srellik found herself stared down. Finally, her spiny, emerald neck frill snapped shut and she hissed, "Fine. I'll take you *camping*."

"I told you she really wanted to go," the Lintar boasted.

The four friends negotiated the schedule and supplies over a final round of drinks for the evening. The Woaoo offered to pack meals for everyone, but they ended up deciding it would be best if they each packed their own rations and other necessities individually. They would meet at the Srellik's docked ship two days hence. They were all excited, but the Woaoo could hardly even wait.

FOUR ALIENS in the cramped crew quarters of a cargo-hauler spaceship, even when the spaceship has cutting edge elasti-drive engines that will keep the trip short, can feel a bit crowded.

The Woaoo was too polite to complain about the tempera-ture that the Srellik kept her ship, but the Heffen wasn't. Any creature with a full coat of fur would be far too hot under the Srellik's blazing heat lamps, and he made sure everyone on board knew that before the end of the first hour. Besides, it made him think of the blasting heat of the last few months, under a growing red sun, before he'd had to join in the evacua-tion of his home world.

The Lintar liked the heat. He kept bobbling about, zipping from one end of the ship to the other, babbling away giddily from the boost the heat gave his cold-blooded body. If the Woaoo and the Heffen hadn't been so irritable, they might have found his behavior amusing. As it was, the Srellik and the heat-weary Woaoo had to intercede several times over the course of the daylong flight to keep the Heffen and the Lintar from coming to blows.

They were all relieved when the Woaoo home world came into view—a glowing ball of white-speckled green and blue hanging in the star-studded blackness. The Srellik piloted her ship down, under the Woaoo's direction, to the very spot in the forests outside Tway-wa-a City where the Woaoo's family used to camp. It was a stretch of forest owned by a distant uncle, and no one was likely to be there, except during the Woaoo Festival of Conformation during the autumn equinox.

It was night when they landed. The Woaoo stepped out of the ship and onto the earthy ground of her home world for the first time in many years. She flexed her claws, feeling the grit of the dirt under them. She sniffed the air and smelled a musky scent that she'd only ever smelled in this forest. It smelled like childhood.

"The trees aren't whistling," the Heffen said, joining her on the ground. His angular ears were twisting about in every direction. "You said they whistled."

"It's almost morning," the Woaoo whispered. "You can tell when the sun's about to rise..." Her voice was reverent and so low that the Heffen could barely hear her. "Because the trees only whistle at night."

The Srellik broke the mood, hissing from behind them, "It's probably a photosynthesis by-product being released through gas valves in the leaves. No big deal really. Lots of plants whistle. Now, where do we build this *campfire?*"

The Lintar had followed the rest of them out by now, but he hung in the air, eerily still, after his antics onboard the warm ship. "I have to agree," he voiced with his thick-lipped mouth. "It's quite cold out here. It makes me feel like hibernating. "

"Cold!" the Woaoo exclaimed. "It's the middle of summer! I can tell by the flowers..." She gazed at the riots of orange and purple nightblooms as if the mere sight of them was a portal back to childhood.

The Heffen squinted. "You can see colors in this dark?" he asked. His night vision must not have been as good as hers.

The Lintar, however, blanched. His normally luminous cerulean skin turned quite white. "I'll freeze!" he said.

The Woaoo got to work on the campfire.

Both of her coldblooded friends were much more cheerful once they felt the warmth of its blaze. Until the sun rose, the Woaoo taught traditional campfire songs from her childhood to the Lintar which they sang in eerie, beautiful duet. The Srellik experimented with burning local flora. Some of the purple flowers blazed quite spectacularly, throwing off bursts of sparks. The orange flowers only fizzled, and they smelled terrible.

All the while, the Heffen sat silently, as morose and reticent as he'd been back on Crossroads Station. The Woaoo watched him while she sang, wondering what he thought.

The fire burned down to embers. The sky lightened, and the day warmed up around them. "Well, show us around your forest," the Lintar said finally. "We've come light-years to see it."

So, the Woaoo led her friends away from the remains of their campfire and out of the clearing that the Srellik's ship had landed in, bushwhacking her way through the underbrush. "I haven't been here since I was a joey," the Woaoo said, pushing a branch aside, "But, there should be a lake this way... And caves I used to play in." Her memory didn't fail her, and the Woaoo had no trouble leading the way. She hoped that the sense of childhood fun and adventure imbued in the very trees around them would soften the Heffen. Bring a little comfort to his heart. Of course, to him the trees were only trees. And alien ones at that. The memories the Woaoo saw imbued in them were actually etched in her memories, not their leaves and bark.

At the lake, the Lintar decided to brave the coldness of the water to enjoy the change in atmosphere. While he wandered around the bottom of the lake wearing diving weights, the Srellik and the Woaoo went spelunking. The very walls and shape of the caves brought the Woaoo back in time to a younger self playing hide-and-seek. Only now, instead of other Woaoo joeys, her playmate was a reptilian alien whose species had evolved on a planet on the other side of the galaxy.

The Heffen sat beside the lake and waited.

When the yellow sun was centered over the sky, the four friends reconvened for lunch. They each picnicked on their own provisions. Being widely disparate species, they mainly did not enjoy or even have the ability to digest the same foods. However, the Woaoo was able to pick and share a few berries with the Heffen. His diet was generally more carnivorous than hers, but he politely, albeit unenthusiastically, accepted her offering of local flavor.

The Srellik sampled her own version of local flavor by zapping an insect hive with her stun gun. The glittering white arthropods she captured were wriggly and then crunchy. She declared them entirely to her liking.

"How long can we stay?" the Woaoo asked.

The Lintar stretched out his body, making his face very long. "How long would you like to stay?" he asked.

The Srellik's emerald neck frill flared. "I have a cargo run on the first of the week," she hissed. "We have to be back for that."

"Two more days, then. That will be fine," the Woaoo said. If that wasn't enough time for this childhood wonderland to soften the Heffen's hard heart, then no time would be.

The Heffen searched the Woaoo's face for hints of disappointment, but he didn't see any. He didn't know that she was more interested in his feelings than the forest. She made so little sense to him.

After the lunch things were cleared away, the Srellik and the Lintar decided to engage in a tree climbing competition. The Lintar, obviously, had the edge, since he had only to empty his air bladder to float up to the treetops. The Srellik, however, being a stubborn individual, enjoyed the challenge of an impossible task, and the Lintar, being a sanguine individual, enjoyed winning, even if it bore little to no reflection on his own skill.

So, the Srellik flexed her green scaled muscles and scrambled about the upper echelons of the trees, while the Lintar bobbled about her like a silky blue cloud. The two warmbloods watched.

"Is it like your world?" the Woaoo asked the Heffen.

"No," he said. One of his ears flicked. "Nothing ever will be." Then he gazed at the Woaoo with his piercing brown eyes. "Will you stay here when we leave? I'm sure you could take on a new identity, leave your artist self behind, and blend back into Woaoo society."

The Woaoo blinked. "I suppose... I could." It was true that since her exile, she'd almost entirely stopped painting. So, there wouldn't be much of her artist's self left to give up.

"Why wouldn't you?" the Heffen pressed, almost angry that the Woaoo would willingly spurn her home world by returning to Crossroads Station when he ached for his own home world so much. "You said you couldn't afford the price of a ticket back... Now, you're back. You said you missed it here. Now, you're here."

"True," she said, discomfited by the Heffen's anger. He was finally directing an emotion at her... and it was the wrong one. She combed long, blunt claws through the silvery tufts of her ears, trying to regain her composure. "But then... I wouldn't be able to afford a ticket home," she said. "To the station, I mean. I have a life there. A career that satisfies me. And friends."

"At least you get to choose," the Heffen said bitterly. "An impossible choice, perhaps, but a choice no less."

The Woaoo reached a small gray paw out gingerly and laid it on the back of the Heffen's large ruddy paw. His fur felt silky against her paw pads. "It's not impossible," she said. "It's not even hard."

The Heffen's breath caught in his throat at the horror of what the Woaoo was saying. How could she dare to turn her back on her home? He turned his wolfish face away. Then he pulled his paw away too.

"I may have missed these forests," the Woaoo said gently. "But my home isn't a planet anymore."

"Right," the Heffen barked angrily. "It's a hollow cylinder of metal floating in space. *That is not a home!*" He stomped off into the forest, crashing noisily through the underbrush, before he could hear the Woaoo's answer.

"You're right," she whispered. "Crossroads Station *isn't* a home." It was too hard to say in front of him—what if he didn't say it in return?—but she said it to the emptiness he'd left around her: "My home is you."

The Heffen hiked through the forests alone until long after the trees began their nightly whistling. The Woaoo, knowing that he needed space, stayed away. She joined the Lintar and Srellik, and they continued climbing trees all afternoon. Then, at dusk, the three of them built a fire and sang songs again. The Srellik had even brought a gummy confection to roast over the flames that puffed up as it heated. All three of them could eat it, since it was composed of only the simplest sugars.

The fire had almost burned out when the Heffen finally joined his friends, having worn his anger out with hiking. They were already sleeping. It was the silence just before dawn, and there were only embers of the merry evening left. He stared at the crimson sparks and thought about how alien the Woaoo's world was to him.

The trees, the bushes, the washed out yellow color of the sky. He'd spent hours that day trying to imagine finding a new home on this world or another like it. For wouldn't it be better to live on a planet—even an alien one like this—than inside the anti-septic metal box called Crossroads Space Station? But he simply could not reconcile himself to the profoundly alien quality of everything around him. The space station he lived on might not be his home... But this wasn't either.

Yet... He looked at the Woaoo sleeping by the embers of the fire. She had had grown up here, evolved here, *belonged* here... He'd never have met her or anyone like her on his long gone home world, but she was not alien. She was his good friend.

The familiar sheen of her downy gray fur tipped with silver

heaved lightly with her breathing. He remembered the touch of her paw from early that afternoon, and, he was suddenly struck by the image of her staying behind when the others left. It's what he would do, if it were his home world.

Despite her protestations, he had trouble believing that she could really leave her home world to return to the cold bulk of a space station. The more he thought about it, the more his chest began to ache with the unbearable thought of his life there without her. If he'd thought Crossroads Station was cold before, it would be infinitely colder if she didn't return.

Almost before he realized what he was doing, the Heffen had curled his larger body around hers. Red fur against gray. He felt her warmth, cuddly and small beside him. The Woaoo sighed in her sleep but didn't awake.

The Srellik and the Lintar found their friends that way in the morning. In whispered hisses of conversation, they agreed to leave the warmbloods to themselves, setting off for an exclusively coldblooded hike.

When the Woaoo finally awoke, she was afraid to move. It might break the spell, and end her dream of strong Heffen arms around her. Yet, her consciousness was catching, and the Heffen soon began to rouse. He started to pull away, but the Woaoo cuddled against his chest, turning her face into the thick red fur.

In the warm delirium of receding unconsciousness, the Heffen responded to her signal, squeezing her in close to him. "Today's your last day," he said, touching his muzzle to her neck. He was almost sure she'd contradict him, and explain that she'd decided to stay in this distressingly alien land. When the words didn't come, he said, "What do you want to do today?"

She still wouldn't look at him. Still afraid to break the spell and send her Heffen back to being the solitary, distant creature he'd always been before. Noble. Unreachable. Lost in his past.

"What did you do on your last day?" the Woaoo asked him. "The day you had to leave your world."

The Heffen sighed, remembering the pain. "I waited in line for hours on the pavement of an airfield full of space cruisers. I had one suitcase, and it was packed so full my arms hurt carrying it." He remembered the pain in his tired arms abstractly, but he couldn't feel it now. All he could feel was the softness of the Woaoo's fur pressed against him.

"Let's not do that," the Woaoo said.

"No," he agreed.

Finally, she pushed away from his shaggy chest and looked up at his strongly articulated, canine face.

"I'm sorry I won't get to visit your planet," she said. He frowned, and she quickly hurried on. "But, I moved away from my planet because I couldn't find what I was looking for here... I didn't know why I couldn't. Until I met you."

The Heffen grumbled a little, deep in his throat, but then he nuzzled his muzzle against the Woao's rounded face, touching his pointed nose to her broad one. He didn't say anything, but the Woaoo could read his heart. They knew each other that well. Across species; across independent yet convergent genetic evolution; across solar systems; and across the galaxy. They'd found each other, and that was home.

The Woaoo spent the final day of their vacation leading the Heffen around the forests she'd explored in her youth. She showed him everything she could remember, from the place where she'd once caught a photosynthetic amphibian with her bare paws to the tree where she used to sit and daydream about outer space. It was like she was trying to reanimate and archive as much of her childhood as possible in his memory so that she wouldn't have to remember it alone. She felt like a joey again.

For his part, the Heffen found his jealousy waning over the Woaoo's ability to revisit the home of her youth. It clearly energized her to share her memories with him... But they were only memories. The thing that was alive and vibrant here was *her*. Not the past she was ineffectually trying to share with him. He could never be a part of that any more than he could return to his own past, but he could be a part of her future.

It was strange to take his eyes off the past he'd lost and look forward. But that's what he did. He saw a life with this cheerful, chittery little Woaoo brightening his every day. As she had done for years, even though he hadn't noticed it.

At twilight, when the trees began whistling, the four friends gathered at the edge of the clearing where the Srellik had parked her spaceship. They built their final campfire, and the Lintar and Woaoo babbled incessantly to each other about all the great things they'd each done all day. The Heffen listened quietly, waiting for everyone to settle down to sleep so he could hold his Woaoo close to him again.

The Srellik listened quietly too. Occasionally, her emerald neck frill flicked out in a collar around her neck the way it sometimes did when she was tallying up the value of a cargo haul, deciding if it was worth the down payment.

"I guess, we'll leave when the trees go quiet in the dark before morning," the Lintar said. His swim-bladder was filled to the point that his delicate blue fins were dragging on the ground, and his O-shaped mouth looked sad.

"Yes," the Srellik agreed, flicking her forked tongue. "We'll be back on Crossroads Station in less than twenty-four hours."

"Then we'd better get some sleep," the Heffen said, gruffly impatient.

Each of them settled into their own portable sleeping nests, beside the dying fire. After a few minutes, the Heffen surreptitiously moved over and cuddled himself up against the Woaoo like he had the night before. Again, she sighed as she felt his warm fur press against her back.

A FEW MINUTES LATER, before any of them had fallen asleep, but while they were all lost in their own quiet thought-worlds in the dark, the Srellik hissed, "In three months, I'll have time to do a trip like this again."

The Lintar chuckled, burping gas from his swim-bladder. He bobbed a foot higher above the ground, his fins trailing gracefully and his gauzy sleep-nest thoroughly disrupted. "I knew it," he said. "*Dirtballs are for pre-tech savages*," he mimicked back in the Srellik's voice mockingly. "Admit it! *You enjoyed yourself.* Shall we make the trip a whole week next time?"

"Maybe next time," the Woaoo said into the darkness, speaking to the Lintar, "you could show us your world. Imagine it—all of us, *except you*, wearing breathing helmets for a change. You must have a fascinating world..." The Heffen squeezed her, showing his approval for the optimistic sense of adventure that the Woaoo brought into his life.

They listened in the dark for the Srellik's answer. When she didn't give one, however, they didn't worry. They all knew anyway. Mentally, she was making plans to arrange for a whole week off. And three sets of breathing gear.

10

WELCOME TO OB'GLAUNG

WATER SPLASHED into the Ob'glaung Station airlock, wetting three sets of feet—a pair of red-furred paws belonging to a Heffen, a pair of gray-tufted paws belonging to a Woaoo, and a pair of green-scaled S'rellick talons. A long blue fin hovered, trailing over the water's surface, as an icthyoid Lintar swam eager circles through the air.

Soon, all of the air would be replaced with liquid atmosphere, and the four aliens would be able to enter the station. Three of them would need to don breathing gear, but the Lintar would be able to take his off for the first time in months. He had grown up on Ob'glaung Station.

The reptilian S'rellick lifted her spike-ridged tail, keeping the rising water off of its green scales a little longer, and hissed at the liquid that would soon surround her.

The Woaoo and Heffen, both furry mammalians, shared a glance in response to their reptilian friend's finicky aversion to the new atmosphere. What did she have to worry about with getting wet? No fur. Then the Woaoo reached one of her tufted gray paws out and clasped the Heffen's red paw. He pulled her in close, and they embraced as the water rose around them.

The final alien in the group—the blue-finned Lintar— could hover above the water, floating due to the ultra-light gases in his swim-bladder. He bobbled about excitedly, soundlessly clapping his elegantly long, silky fins. He had brought his friends to the space station where he'd grown up to celebrate his hatch-day. "It's time to put your breathing helmets on," he said, diving down to the rising surface of the water. "And take mine off!" He submerged, and a moment later, the bubble-like helmet he always wore bobbed back up to the surface.

The water was now waist-high on the koala-like Woaoo and thigh-high on the taller wolf-like Heffen; the reptilian S'rellick had decided to bite the bullet and plunge in neck-deep by kneeling down. She could see her icthyoid friend swimming circles around her under the wavery surface of the water atmosphere. She shook her head and then affixed her breathing gear over her face.

The Heffen and Woaoo followed suit, and then all three friends plunged under the water.

The Lintar blinked his wide fish-eyes at them. "Welcome!" he intoned. None of them had ever seen the Lintar without his breathing helmet before. In all of the years of their friendship, travelling together as a group, they'd never seen him without his helmet on. The sleek lines of his narrow body were sinuous and unbroken without the clunky mechanical bubble over his head. He looked natural. And happy.

The airlock finished cycling atmospheres, and all four of them were left floating in a small room filled with water. The artificial gravity shut off, and the internal doors slid open, revealing the stunning sight of the water-filled space station of Ob'glaung.

The Woaoo, Heffen, and S'rellick watched as their Lintar friend swam dartingly out of the airlock like a streak of blue lightning. He became one of many Lintars and other water-breathing aliens swimming in the thick atmosphere of Ob'glaung. Many were different forms of icthyoids, some were tentacled, others had calcareous shells or chitinous exoskeletons, and even a few seemed to be bulbous, blubbery mammal-like creatures—sentient water-breathing whales or manatees or some such.

All through the scene in front of them, strands of bioluminescent kelp wavered in the wakes of swimming passersby. Far off in the distance, they could make out a curving translucent horizon that looked back out on the star-studded void of space. From the outside, Ob'glaung looked like a shimmering dewdrop hanging in the dark. Inside, Ob'glaung was a giant busy pond, and every direction was up. It didn't need to simulate gravity by rotating like a wheel station, since all of its inhabitants were already used to a life of floating.

The S'rellick was the first to attempt following her Lintar friend away from the airlock. Her long reptilian tail swayed back and forth, making her a decent swimmer. The Woaoo and Heffen, on the other hand, were pathetically awkward trying to navigate an atmosphere unnaturally thick and multi-directional for them. Their fuzzy limbs sprawled and splayed, dragging them sadly and slowly along. Nonetheless, they managed to catch up to their friends—the Lintar and the S'rellick—since those two were kind enough to wait for them.

"So, what do you guys want to do?" the Lintar asked. His voice was picked up by the sound-sensors in the others' breathing gear and translated into sound-waves they could interpret in the bubbles of atmosphere around each of their heads.

"Your voice sounds so close this way..." the Woaoo said. "It's strange having my head inside a bubble."

"Yeah," the Heffen woofed. "How do you not feel claustrophobic all the time?"

The icthyoid shrugged his long elegant fins, drifting sideways. "It makes me feel kind of safe, actually."

"What do you mean, 'what do we want to do?'" the S'rellick asked in her usual sarcasm. "This is your hatch-day celebration, on the space station you grew up on. Shouldn't you have a plan for what we're going to do here?"

The Lintar turned one way and then the other, looking around the place that he had once called home. But it wasn't his home anymore. And it hadn't been for a long time. He had wanted to return, but it had been for sentimental reasons, not practical ones. Simply being here, sharing it with the people he was closest to, soothed something deep inside. It made him feel like his friends knew him better. But he didn't have a plan, not beyond coming here. "There's a reason I moved to Crossroads Station," he finally said. "I never fit in here. I never really knew what to do."

"You mean..." the Woaoo couldn't resist, but she also couldn't stop herself from giggling as she said it, "...that you felt like a fish out of water?"

"Yes," the Lintar said without the slightest hint of levity. He stared levelly at his three dearest friends—a green lizard, a red-wolf, and a fluffy little koala—each of them floating awkwardly and wearing a diving helmet, obscuring their natural faces. This must be how he looked to them all the time. Obscured.

But he was okay with that. The Lintar's diving helmet had started to feel like part of who he was. And his friends knew who he was on the inside, regardless of whether he hid his face in a bubble of tech. It was liberating to shed it... but it was also strange.

The S'rellick could see that the Lintar had lost himself in thought. That happened to him a lot. The four aliens had travelled to many worlds together, and explored many places that had been new to all four of them. They knew each other very well. "Tell you what," she said. "Let's go explore this place together."

"That sounds wonderful," the Lintar said. But first, he darted back into the airlock and fetched his breathing helmet from where it floated. He clipped it to a buckle on the utility harness he wore. He'd be needing it again later.

11

ONE ALIEN'S WRECKAGE

CHORIF'S ROUND feathered face stared down at the contents of the cryo-pod, and her wide copper eyes narrowed. She had been expecting to find valuable cargo for salvage; instead, all she saw was a squirmy green-fleshed larva, about the length of Chorif's upper wing.

"Anything in there?" Amy called out. She was another space-wreck scavenger.

Usually, Chorif didn't like to share her finds, but Amy's cruiser had arrived seconds before her own at the charred remains of this shuttle, smashed into asteroid 835. So, Chorif had puffed up her breast feathers, squawked a good story about avian authority in this sector, and been relieved when Amy agreed to share the find rather than insist on her rightful claim.

"It's just a larval version of the lepidopteran aliens who owned this vessel," Chorif chuffed.

"It's their kid?" Amy said, pushing Chorif aside to see the larva for herself. The pink skin between her small blue eyes creased. "Damn. An orphan now."

Chorif grasped one end of the cryo-chamber with her strong, lower wings and said, "You want this? Or can I have it?

Either way, it's a heavy piece of equipment, so we should move it together. We can dump the larva out and leave it in the wreckage."

"Are you kidding?" Amy said.

Chorif's owlish eyes blinked. "No? I mean, it won't be dangerous to us. Look at it." Following her own advice, Chorif looked down at the helpless green caterpillar-like thing again. It kind of made her hungry. If it were smaller—say, only a talon's-length long—and she had a whole bowlful of them...

Chorif clacked her beak hungrily.

"It'll die," Amy said. Chorif wasn't terribly familiar with human tonal communication, but Amy's voice had raised in pitch and taken on... an irritating quality.

"If you're worried about cruelty," Chorif conceded, raising a talon toward the larva, "I suppose I can kill it now so that it won't suffer from starvation."

Before Chorif could close her claws on the larva, Amy's pink-skinned fingers darted out and scooped it up. She cradled the caterpillar-like creature in her arms, rocking it and making low cooing sounds to it.

"Such smooth skin," Amy said. Looking up at Chorif, she asked, "Is this really a larval version of the aliens we saw crushed in the cockpit? It's going to grow huge, colorful wings like that?"

Chorif nodded, unsure what was happening here.

"Amazing," Amy breathed, staring down at the caterpillar-creature in her arms again. "You're going to be beautiful," she said.

Was the human actually talking to the infant larva? Amazing, Chorif thought. Apparently, the human valued this alien baby. How odd. Suddenly, a thought struck Chorif: "Hey, I'll trade you the larva for the cryo-pod."

As addled as the human seemed by the presence of an alien baby, she still shot Chorif a look that meant she could see right through that gambit. "No doing. You were going to leave it here, so I get it for free. Trade something else for the cryo-chamber."

Chorif grumbled. She was really off her game today.

But at least she wasn't as crazy as this human.

Amy wandered out of the crashed ship's cargo bay, back to the docking port, and onto her own ship where she called up a viewscreen and immediately sent a vid-message to Crossroads station, all while bouncing the squirming larva on her hip: "This is Salvager 41, and I've found a survivor in the wreckage on asteroid 835. An infant. Could you search the databases and send me any information about whether anyone's looking for this infant? Anyone I can return it to? Any information about custody, really. Thanks and out."

Chorif chittered. She'd followed the human out of curiosity, and now it all made sense. "You're going to hold it for ransom?" she asked, admiringly.

Before Amy could answer, the viewscreen lit up with an image of a reptilian alien. "Salvager 41, we've checked the records, and the crashed shuttle on asteroid 835 was registered to a Lei-ca-thor, a species that doesn't have a centralized representation in the Expansion. They show up as traders and cargo-haulers occasionally, but there's no one for us to contact regarding this matter. If you bring the infant to us, we can enroll it in the fosterage. Otherwise, under salvage rights, you can claim it as your own. However, you will be expected to pass several examinations regarding your fitness as an adoptive parent to an alternate species before the arrangement can be made permanent. Over and out."

Chorif chuckled at how the human's plan had back-fired on her. The upward curve to her fleshy lips was clearly an expression of her disappointment.

"I think I'll name you Lee-a-lei," Amy said.

12

THE CROWDS ON CROSSROADS STATION

Roscoe's velvety nose twitched, but his long ears stood tall in spite of his jittery nerves. The view of Crossroads Station on the viewscreen was intimidating: three concentric wheels, rotating in alternating directions, each one lined with row after row of glowing windows. Shuttle pods and star cruisers of all designs were docked on the outer ring.

Roscoe had never felt small before. Well, certainly, he was literally small—only half the height of High Royal Quejon whom he served, but then all the members of his race of uplifted lapines were smaller than the grand elven primates who'd uplifted them.

Still! Roscoe served a High Royal! And the court he served on was the foremost in their solar system! Except now Roscoe realized, for the first time, what it meant when High Royal Quejon talked about an entire galaxy of other solar systems...

"Can you establish contact?" High Royal Quejon asked from her throne-like passenger seat in their—suddenly small-seeming—two-man spacecraft. It was a top-of-the-line model in their own solar system.

Roscoe worked the controls and managed to pull up a video

display on the viewscreen of a brightly-colored, broad-shouldered, mechanical biped. "Welcome to Crossroads Station," it said. "Would you like to be assigned a docking port?"

Roscoe glanced over his shoulder to see High Royal Quejon frowning her slender lips. "I thought this was a *human* station," she said. "Why am I talking to a robot?"

The colorful metal man said, "Crossroads Station is technically a terran outpost, yes. However, many species live and work here. Right now, I'm working the dock assignments. Would you like one?"

"Yes," Roscoe said, eagerly. He knew he'd outstepped his place, but he was suddenly very excited about seeing the insides of Crossroads Station. So, he accepted the robot's docking assignment, and once the video communication was turned off, he listened obsequiously to High Royal Quejon's reprimands while carefully docking the ship.

High Royal Quejon agreed that the best plan at this point was to board the station and seek out the leaders of the human government in person. After finishing the docking procedures, the two of them debarked their small ship's airlock.

On the other side, an entirely new kind of world opened up to Roscoe. Giant curved windows far above Roscoe's tall ears let him see the inner wheels of the station rotating in the star-studded sky. All around him, crowds and throngs of various aliens milled and lumbered and strolled and charged about. Some were feathered, others scaled, and many had fur like him. The tallest alien he could see had a long, curving neck and feathered wing-like arms. The most common type, though, were about twice Roscoe's height with angular muzzles, triangular ears, and ruddy red fur.

The only aliens that interested High Royal Quejon though were the primatoids that looked like shorter, thicker versions of herself. She pointed at one of them and said, "There, that one's a human." She looked down at Roscoe and added, "Go arrange a diplomatic meeting for me."

Roscoe hopped over to the human and said nervously in the Solanese he'd learned for the occasion, "Excuse me, but I serve the High Royal Quejon of Ourouri System. We're here to make diplomatic connections with the Human Expansion."

The human gave Roscoe a quizzical look. He recognized it as quizzical, because the human really did look a lot like High Royal Quejon, except for rounder ears, broader features, and a shock of fur on top of its head. Also, looking at the human closer, Roscoe realized that its skin was truly bare; High Royal Qujon's skin was covered with a fine downy fur.

"I'm just a tourist," the human said. "So, I don't know my way around either. Good luck though."

Roscoe watched the human amble off, just one of the crowd, no more or less important than the feathered, scaled, and furred aliens all around. Then Roscoe looked back at the ruler he'd been serving his entire life. Her posture was stiff and awkward. Her long jeweled robes looked out of place. She was lost here.

But for once, Roscoe felt right at home. He knew better than to wave goodbye as he disappeared into the crowds on Crossroads Station.

13

PRINCIPLES OVER PROFIT

CHORIF HELD out her upper wing, spreading her feathers to admire the rings and bracelets and pins she'd fastened among her pinions. Her wing glittered with gems from the ice asteroids around Tau Ceti and glowed with Erdidaniian opals. She looked like a queen, and she clacked her hooked beak happily.

All of the salvage crews based out of Crossroads Station had been searching for the lost High Royal Quejon's vessel for months, but only Chorif had thought to seek out the uplifted lapine servant who'd run away from the Quejon and enlist his services.

For a split of the take, Roscoe had agree to come along with Chorif as first mate and provide useful pearls of knowledge. For instance, Roscoe had known that his previous master could barely drive her own spacecraft and had a superstitious fear of ringed planets and gas giants.

Following the nervous, long-eared alien's advice, Chorif had piloted her salvage vessel along an extremely inefficient path out of the Crossroads Station system, missing out on all the potential gravity boosts, and finally ended up here: at a rogue, wandering planet in the darkness between star systems.

The High Royal Quejon must have crashed her ship on the dark planet and then abandoned it in an automatic homing escape pod. That meant, when the High Royal Quejon eventually made it back to her homeworld, they'd know where to look for the crashed vessel; its location would be stored in the escape pod's data banks.

Of course, a sub-lightspeed escape pod with its passenger in stasis could take years to get home. Until then, only Chorif and Roscoe knew where the High Royal Quejon's vessel had crashed... along with its cargo load of lovely, shimmering jewels.

Roscoe slipped several bangley gold bracelets over his long ears, and they settled on his head like funny, lopsided crowns. His nose twitched, and his fuzzy muzzle curled into a grin. "I always wanted to try these on."

"The Quejon didn't let you?" Chorif placed an actual tiara among the fluffy feathers of her head. This was the most fun she'd had with a salvage operation since she'd had the fortune of watching a baker's catering vessel crash right into an asteroid. Aldebaran sugar tarts and Cygni flower bud eclairs, seven tier cakes, all of it delicious and all of it ruined—lightly smashed, but perfectly fresh. Of course, it hadn't been at all profitable. But very tasty.

"I never asked," Roscoe said, ears drooping over their gold adornments. "Never dared defy her at all until I saw the crowds on Crossroads Station—so many different alien species, all mixed up together, living as equals."

"Some more equal than others," Chorif chirped, admiring the gems dripping off of her upper wings again.

"More equal than on my homeworld." The lapine draped a silver beaded necklace over his chest; it shimmered like a waterfall. "My species was uplifted from feral animals by the Quejon's primatoid species; they evolved sentience naturally. And they'll never let us forget it."

"If they're serious about joining the Expansionist Consortium," Chorif cawed, starting to take off her jewels, "then they might. Why do you think the Quejon was bringing these jewels home?"

Roscoe shrugged his narrow, furry shoulders.

"She couldn't buy her way in with them."

Roscoe looked down at the gems and jewelry around him with a new expression. Quizzical. Uncertain. "You think the Quejon brought these to the humans on Crossroads Station to buy a diplomatic relationship and was turned down?"

Chorif pulled the last ring off her longest pinion and smoothed down her ruffled feathers. "That would be my guess."

"The Quejon has never been turned down for anything..." Roscoe's words were slow and reverent as he savored the idea of his former master being denied something she wanted, something she assumed she deserved.

"All right," Chorif said, clacking her beak. "We've had our fun; time to put the jewelry away."

"Do you have a buyer for it or something?" Roscoe asked, slipping the bracelets back off of his ears.

Chorif tilted her head, staring Roscoe down with her wide, round avian eyes. "We're turning it in."

"Wait, what?" Roscoe's long ears stood bolt upright in surprise. "We're giving it back?! The reward for returning it can't be a fraction of what its actually worth!" He held a pawful of the bracelets possessively against his chest.

"It's not," Chorif agreed. "But my reputation is, and if I sell this stuff on the black market, I'll lose my salvage license with Crossroads Station." She held out her lower wings toward Roscoe, expecting the lapine to hand over his hoard of gold bangles.

Reluctantly, Roscoe handed the bracelets over, and Chorif

packed them back into the cargo crate where they'd found them. She hoisted the repacked crate up with her strong lower wings and asked, "So is there anything else on this vessel of value? Any good equipment?"

Roscoe showed her around the small vessel, pointing out anything that might be valuable. None of it was. And soon the two temporary partners were back on Chorif's salvage vessel, flying back towards Crossroads Station.

Chorif usually salvaged alone, so she was used to flying in silence. But Roscoe's subdued demeanor seemed out of character after his earlier chattiness. Regardless, Chorif continued with the routine part of her work—piloting home, accepting a docking assignment from the colorful, broad-shouldered robot who appeared on the viewscreen, and then informing him of their successful find.

As the airlock cycled, Roscoe finally spoke: "You really trust the Crossroads Station government." He was staring at her appraisingly, nose twitching intermittently.

"No," Chorif chirped. "But this is my home, and working with them is better than the alternative. I know you just ran away from your entire life, but I have a life here. I don't want to run away from it just because I found a box of sparkly gemstones."

"You could be rich somewhere else," Roscoe said.

The airlock finished cycling, and the outer door opened to the crowded docking quarter of Crossroads Station. Chorif hoisted up the cargo crate again with her lower wings. As the avian and lapine walked out into the crowds of all different sorts of aliens, Chorif gestured with her upper wings at the bustle and happy noise all around them. "Where else?" she cawed. "This is where I live. No amount of being rich is better than that."

Roscoe hopped along beside Chorif. He wasn't sure he

agreed with her. He hadn't been living on Crossroads Station that long yet. But it gave him hope about his new home that a cynical avian like Chorif loved it enough to choose principles over profit to stay here.

14

INALIENABLE RIGHTS

Roscoe's long ears would not stand tall, no matter how he strained to hold them up. His reflection in the empty viewscreen looked haggard and scared, but he'd stared at it for long enough trying to compose himself. He would never be composed. He had to proceed anyway.

With a nervous twitch of his nose, Roscoe opened a communication channel to the planet below, and moments later, a familiar face filled the viewscreen: his cousin Chilchi. Her ears stood tall.

"Roscoe! We thought we'd never see you again! It's been three years!"

Roscoe's nerves calmed a little at the warm sight of his cousin. "Can you put me through to the High Royal Quejon?"

"Of course," Chilchi said, suddenly all business.

Roscoe felt bad rebuffing her like that, but he had to do the hard part of this first. There would be time to catch up later—if he could get through the hard part. If he could stand up to the High Royal.

Chilchi's fuzzy, round, lapine face disappeared from the screen and was replaced by the long, narrow face of the High

Royal Quejon. Her fur was as fine and pale as dandelion down, and her primatoid features were pinched and creased. Her black eyes burned like the void.

"You are dead to me, runaway bunny." The High Royal Quejon spat the words, as if it was beneath her to speak to a former slave at all.

"I am free from you," Roscoe corrected, finding his voice in spite of his nerves. He had feared this day for years, and yet the Quejon wasn't nearly so scary to behold as he remembered. She was twice his height, he remembered, but on the screen she looked small. He had bested her once before, escaping into the crowds on Crossroads Station to become a free lapine. Now he would best her again.

"I've come back to free my family," Roscoe said, ears straightening proudly above him. He transmitted a list down to the surface, containing every extended family member and friend he'd ever had—one hundred some uplifted lapine slaves in all.

The High Royal Quejon frowned as she read the transmission. "This is every one of my servants, many of my compatriots' servants, and some servants that have been traded into different keeps during the last several years."

"I'll also need the spouses and children of anyone on that list," Roscoe added.

"You can't seriously expect me to hand this many uplifted lapines over. Even if you could afford them, as a runaway, you have no standing for purchasing them. Furthermore, my keep couldn't handle this level of upheaval. I could never part with this many well trained servants for any price."

Roscoe's ears didn't waver as he said, "I'm not buying them." He'd already spent all of the money he'd saved during the last three years to rent this starship—a vessel large enough to ferry all of them back to Crossroads Station. "I'm offering free transport to them."

"On their behalf, I turn you down."

"I don't recommend that." Roscoe's fuzzy face had never looked less cute. He was a lapine ready to fight. He would give no quarter to this primatoid who had owned the first half of his life. "Enslavement of sentient beings—evolved, uplifted, manufactured, or otherwise—is a crime of the first order in the Western Spiral Arm Treaty Alliance."

The High Royal Quejon's ears were too small to splay, but the look in her black eyes was priceless. She was cornered, and she knew it.

"You knew about that law," Roscoe said, piecing together what had happened three years ago after he'd run away from her. "That's why you went home without joining the alliance. Because you learned about that law, and you decided you'd rather keep my people enslaved."

"We uplifted you!" the Quejon shrieked. "You were feral rabbits until we tweaked your genes, changing you over generations." Her long-fingered hands balled into fists, and her black eyes flashed like stars collapsing. "It was painstaking work. Hard work. You owe us. *You belong to us.*"

"Not according to interstellar law." Roscoe could see the Quejon weighing her options. He only had one ship; he couldn't back up his claim. But if he'd registered his plans with Crossroads Station, then someone might come looking for him if he didn't return. If they came looking for him... No, she had to keep her planet hidden to preserve her way of life.

If she sent him on his way without what he wanted, he could report a massive sentients' rights violation.

If she gave him what he wanted... It might buy her species a few more years, before their entire way of life was overturned.

"You are an ungrateful creature, and we should never have uplifted your kind," the Quejon said. Then her sour primatoid face disappeared.

A moment later, Chilchi reappeared on the viewscreen,

looking bewildered but happy. "I'm told that I have some arrangements to make for you?"

Roscoe's ears couldn't stand any taller as he said, "Let me tell you about where I've been living—it's an interstellar hub called Crossroads Station, and I think you'd like it there."

15

CRESCENT HORNS AND TALL EARS

THE LITTLE LAPINE aliens hopped into the bar, one after the other, noses twitching and long ears swiveling. Narchi had never seen their species in the All Alien Cafe before, and all of a sudden, here were a dozen.

Narchi's heavy hunched shoulders straightened a little at the sight of the group of them. There was something comforting about how they moved together, leaning in to whisper one to the other, all a part of a little herd.

Narchi was a herd alien. At least, she had been. Then those naked-skinned primates and reptilian scientists had come to her homeworld, talking about all the sparkling wonders of the universe, and she couldn't resist. So, she'd hitched a ride and found herself here on Crossroads Station, fifty lightyears from home, and unable to pay for a ride back.

And, sure, it was sparkling out here. There were sentient alien versions of just about every living thing that there'd been back home—right down to the flowers and trees. It was amazing to walk up to a sentient tree, introduce yourself, and then be ignored because the sentient tree had other things to do than talk to a sentient buffalo. It was also painfully lonely. And depressing.

So, Narchi had settled into a pattern of hauling cargo crates around all day—she had the strong back for it—and drinking her loneliness away at the All Alien Cafe while watching the crowds walk by at night. Eventually, she'd earn enough to commission a starhopper to take her back home. Of course, she was sure that if she ever got home to her space-travel world, it would feel small and claustrophobic now, cut off from the smorgasbord of cultures up here in the sky.

So, she tried every drink on the menu once, ate at every little food stand in the merchant quarter, and tried to get to know as many of the aliens around as would make time for her. She wanted to absorb it all.

To that end, Narchi got up from the bar, carrying her bright-orange drink, and went over to the table with the little lapines. They were sitting in a circle, chattering rapidly to each other, but they all quieted down when Narchi loomed over them with her broad shoulders covered in thick, curly, brown fur and her massive head topped with sharp crescent horns.

"May I join you?" Narchi asked.

The little lapines looked at one another, glances darting back and forth, noses twitching furiously, until all of them came to a sort of consensus—all eyes turned to look at the same lapine whose tall ears suddenly drooped, realizing he'd been elected their leader. He looked up at Narchi and said, "We're having a sort of family conference, you see. Otherwise—"

Narchi waited no further. She grabbed a chair from a neighboring table and shoved her way in to the family gathering of rabbit aliens. "I love family conferences," she said, her voice coming out as a much too loud and low bellow. "My family is a long ways away, and I don't get to see them anymore. What are you conferencing about?"

The lapine who'd been elected leader raised one ear to a half-mast flop, intrigued by the big buffalo alien's surprising gregariousness. "We're trying to make a plan for where to live."

"We just got here!" another lapine piped in.

"We need quarters for nearly a hundred," offered another.

Narchi blinked at the dozen rabbit aliens around her. "A hundred?" she asked.

"Oh, we're just the heads-of-family," the unofficial leader said. "The others are over at the nearest playground, letting the kits play, but it's going to be awfully crowded trying to cram a hundred of us into my quarters tonight."

"Your quarters?" Narchi felt a little dizzy talking to these rabbit aliens. They talked a lot faster than her own people. Still, it was awfully nice to be talking to a big family. If she pictured their long ears as horns, they were almost like little versions of her own people.

"Yes," the leader explained. "See, I've been living here for a while, but I only recently saved enough money to fly home and bring the rest of my family out."

Now that made sense to Narchi! Except for the part where his family had willingly come with him... She didn't think anyone else on her homeworld was interested in traveling into space. No matter how interesting it was up here.

Suddenly, though, all the little rabbit aliens began flooding Narchi with stories of their trip and the conditions they'd left on their homeworld. Apparently, unlike Narchi's people, they hadn't evolved on their own, they'd been uplifted by a race of primatoids that enslaved them. Crazy primates. Always causing trouble.

"Look," Narchi said, her bellowing voice breaking into the cacophony of chattering lapines, "it's not much, but if some of you would like to crash in my quarters for a while, you'd be more than welcome."

Twitching noses. And silence.

Embarrassed by her unguarded and unprompted offer, Narchi bellowed on, "I know two sets of quarters won't house a hundred, but it'll come a lot closer than one set. Besides, I think they assigned me bigger than usual quarters here. Cause I'm big. But I don't need the space. In fact, it's kind of lonely."

Looks passed among the rabbit aliens, and the twitching noses slowed. Finally, the unofficially elected leader held a small paw out and said, "My name's Roscoe. And I think you've just found yourself a new family for a while."

Narchi's wide muzzle split into a grin, and she imagined her crescent horns standing taller with pride like the little lapine's ears could. "Believe me," she said, taking the lapine's tiny paw in her broad, hoof-like hand and squeezing it ever so gently, "It's my honor."

16

BLACK OUT IN SPACE

THE LIGHTS HAD GONE OUT ten minutes ago. The sound of the air circulators had shut down too. Narchi didn't know what was happening, but she was scared. Power shouldn't shut down on a space station. Yet, she had to hold herself together. Her lapine roommates had left her babysitting nearly a dozen of their children. When she'd agreed, she hadn't expected it to be in the dark.

Tiny lapines with strong legs and big feet bounced off the walls in their quarters. Literally. Fuzzy bodies rocketed past each other in every which direction, occasionally thudding into the broad thick-hided side of their buffalo-like host. Narchi let out a soft, "Oof!", whenever one of the lapine kits knocked into her, but she didn't mind. Not really.

Narchi had been sharing her quarters with an extended family of uplifted lapines for several months, ever since the rabbit-like sentients had escaped from their homeworld.

So, Narchi was used to a certain amount of frenetic bouncing around her. But usually, it wasn't in the dark. All of her instincts told her that darkness meant stillness. Her species were plains-folk from a planet with five moons. So, she'd never before experienced the type of darkness that happens on a space station during a black out. It was a total darkness, the kind that can only be found deep inside a cave on most planets, and it didn't seem to bother the lapine children. Their species had been uplifted from burrowers.

Narchi wasn't an expert on child-rearing, but bouncing in the dark seemed like the kind of activity that the adult in charge was supposed to stop. Since she was the babysitter right now, that meant her.

With a bellowing, bovine voice, Narchi mooed into the darkness, "Settle down now! No more hopping!"

Lapine giggles erupted around her. The hopping didn't stop. In fact, from the increased fuzzy pummeling of her side, Narchi could only conclude that they'd used her moo as a way to target her in the total dark.

Narchi sighed. This would not do. The little lapines were going to break things, knock over furniture, and hurt themselves if they kept this up. They needed a better activity.

Going against her own instincts, Narchi felt her way through the darkness, moving slowly and touching everything with her hoof-hands to keep from bumping into things. That is, things other than the little lapines, some of whom had clung onto her hunched shoulders for a ride. Finally, she found the drawer where Roscoe, one of the adult lapines, kept his knitting. She pulled out a ball of the Eridanii arachni-silk yarn and started tying loops into it at regular intervals, tricky work in the dark.

Narchi hooked her own hoof-hand through one of the loops, held the knotted mess of yarn out and mooed, "Come over here, little ones. Each of you, find a loop of yarn, and hold on tight with your paw."

A chorus of chirpy voices, assaulted her with questions:

"Why?"

"Is it a game?"

"Are we going somewhere?"

As they questioned her, Narchi felt little tugs on the yarn that meant the lapine children were grabbing the loops. "Yes," she mooed. "We're going on a walk." The lights might be down in their quarters, but there had to be light, at least minimal light, in the more communal parts of Crossroads Station. And if they got out of their darkened quarters, maybe Narchi would have a chance of finding out what was going on.

Before leaving their quarters, Narchi placed her hoof-hand on each of the lapine children's heads in turn, between their long ears. She counted fifteen; that was everyone. "Stay close," she said.

The strange parade—a sentient buffalo followed by more than a dozen sentient bunnies, following her like little ducklings—lumbered and hopped their way down the hallways of Crossroads Station's residential quarter in the dark. Narchi held her loop of yarn with one hoof-hand and trailed the other hoof-hand along the wall, feeling her way.

"I see something!" one of the little lapines squeaked.

Narchi still couldn't see anything, but the lapines' eyes were better than hers. Their ears too. All their senses seemed to be stronger. Sometimes, she felt like a giant dull lump around the bouncy little things.

"I see it too!" a chorus of little lapines cried.

Suddenly, Narchi found herself tugged forward by the yarn as all her little bunny-ducklings hopped towards the dim source of light.

"It's the Merchant Quarter!" one of the lapines chirped. "Can we get Hegulan churros?"

The other children started chirping about all sorts of other treats they wanted to buy, and Narchi realized she'd left her ident card in their quarters. She also realized that she had no idea how to find her way back to their quarters through the dark. "Let's find out what's going on first."

All the little lapines moaned in disappointment.

The Merchant Quarter was extra busy, aliens of all shapes and sizes milling together, staring up at the windows that curved over the wide hallway that was always filled with food stands and vendor stalls.

The stars had never looked so bright. They twinkled in the darkness. The only light came from a few emergency lanterns embedded along the walls, so the entire quarter was trapped in a strange dim twilight.

Narchi gathered her lapine wards in close, counting from one to fifteen repeatedly, checking to make sure none of the long-eared children had strayed.

A double-winged avian alien—an Eechee—approached the funny group and cawed to Narchi, "You look a little over-whelmed."

Several of the lapine children had climbed onto Narchi's wide back again. One of them had climbed all the way up to sit on her shoulders, holding her two crescent horns like handle-bars. "You could say that," Narchi agreed.

"This is Roscoe's family, isn't it?" the Eechie cawed. "I'm Chorif. He's gone on salvage trips with me."

"What happened?" Narchi mooed. "Does anyone know?"

An ursine alien, large and furry like Narchi, heard their conversation and joined in: "I heard it's a space storm."

"An electro-magnetic pulse from a solar flare," offered an orange-furred canine alien, one of the station's most common species.

Somehow the darkness and uncertainty drew everyone together. Aliens who would usually never talk to each other, too busy with their own lives, now had nothing better to do than stand around and speculate about the station-wide power outage.

"How long do you think it will last?" Narchi asked, her head tilting wildly to the side as the lapine on her shoulders decided to try steering her using her horns.

Chorif laughed at the sight, a cackling cawing sound. "You've got your hands full, haven't you? How'd you end up in charge of so many of Roscoe's younger kin?"

The little lapine on Narchi's shoulders piped up: "We share quarters! She watches us when the b'dults are busy!"

"Roscoe and their other parents got a job checking the sound-proofing and acoustics on a recording studio cruiser that belongs to some visiting reptilian pop star," Narchi explained. "Good ears, you know. They left right before the power went out."

"Star Shaker—I love her music," Chorif said, ruffling out the feathers in her lower wings. "I know where her ship's docked. Want me to take you there?"

Narchi eyed the restless little bunnies huddled around her, ears drooping. "I think what we really need is..." She was reluctant to say it around them, but whispering would do no good. Their ears could hear anything she said. "A snack."

Drooping ears perked up, and fifteen little noses started twitching eagerly. "Oh, yes, please," said many little hopeful voices.

A green-skinned amphibian alien with a long snake-like tail instead of legs slithered over and said, "Head over to the grav-bubble playground—the grav-bubble play-structures are down, but all the merchants with quickly perishable food are giving away what they can't sell fast enough."

"Thank you," Narchi said. She knew the way to the playground.

The buffalo led her herd of bunnies through the unusually friendly crowds, accompanied by Roscoe's double-winged avian friend. When they got to the playground, they found that all manner of alien children were playing low-tech games of chase and tag. Merchants of all species plied them with sticky melting frozen treats. For the little ones, a station-wide power outage was heaven.

Now that Narchi's wards were under control and busy playing, she stuffed the Eridanii arachni-silk yarn in her pocket. The terror she'd been holding at bay, inside a knot deep in her stomach, flowed out and filled her body. It hadn't been safe to feel it before now, not with all the little bunnies depending on her. "No one answered any of the real questions while I had fifteen babies clinging to me," Narchi mooed softly to Chorif. "How common is this? How long will it last? Will it get fixed? What happens if it doesn't?"

"You haven't been a citizen of space long, have you?" Chorif cawed, watching the lapines play.

"Less than a year. I was picked up by a passing research team; my species hasn't made it to space on our own yet."

"Power outages in space are rare and bad," Chorif cawed, feathers ruffling all over her body. "To knock a space station like Crossroads out, we're dealing with a one in a million storm. The EM waves had to be powerful enough to blow out everything but the most protected systems; that means even those of us with our own spaceships—I have my own little cargo hauler —can't wake up our ships to get out of here until the storm subsides. Either the waves die down in the next few hours or..."

"Or people stop being nice to each other," Narchi said.

"I don't know about that. If no one has anywhere to go, there's not a lot left to fight over."

The thought settled over them somberly. Narchi wondered if she should take the young ones looking for their parents, so they could all be together. She tried not to think: "die together." The lapines seemed so powerful with their acute senses most of the time, but right now, they seemed small and delicate. Narchi's large body was built for weathering droughts and storms. She didn't want to watch these bunnies die.

She didn't want to die. Suddenly, Narchi wished that she'd sent more radio messages home during the last year.

"I think it's better if we stay here," Narchi said. "The little ones are happy playing. I'm sure Roscoe and the others will find us." On an impulse, Narchi asked her new friend, "Do you have any regrets?"

"Other than being here today instead of on some random lush forest planet?" Chorif cawed, folding her wings up tight.

"Other than that."

"Not a one."

Narchi nodded her heavy buffalo head. "That's a good way to live." And when she thought about it, she didn't really have any regrets either. Not big ones. When given the chance, she'd taken the risk and left her homeworld. She'd seen more of the universe than any other member of her species.

The lights flickered, darker, brighter, darker, and finally all the way out. For a few startling heartbeats, the entire merchant quarter was drowned in velvet darkness, lit only by the twinkling stars.

Then the metal floor hummed under Narchi's hooves, and the entire station vibrated back to life. The lights flashed on, blindingly bright. Cries of childhood despair filled the playground—their power outage adventure was over. But the rest of the merchant quarter gasped, hundreds of individuals letting out a breath of relief as if one.

"How about you?" Chorif cawed. "Any regrets? Cause it looks like you'll have a chance to do something about them."

Fifteen lapine children swarmed the buffalo sentient, tugging at her shaggy fur and hopping around her hooves. "The gravity bubbles are working again! Come play with us!" Just as quickly, they swarmed off and, one by one, hopped into the grav-bubbles to spin and float around the playground.

"I feel like I should have realized something important…"

Narchi scratched at the base of her left crescent horn. "Like it's time to go home. Or to explore the universe further."

Chorif shrugged her upper wings. "Facing death doesn't have to be deep."

"Maybe just that living on a space station isn't safe...?"

Again, the Eechie shrugged, this time with her lower wings. "This storm was one in a million, remember? Is anywhere really safe?"

"I guess not..." Narchi watched the little lapines playing, and all she could think was that it looked fun. And she was happy living on Crossroads Station.

But she was also happy that the power was back on.

17

OF CAKES AND ROBOTS

CHIRRI WATCHED the robot lumber back and forth outside her bakery window for several minutes, seeming undecided, before it came in. Once inside, the metal creature with its dome-shaped head and boxy limbs perused the displays of sugary confections, fancy layered cakes, and simple cookies. Chirri's tufted triangular ears splayed in confusion at the sight. There were lots of robots on Crossroads Station, but none of them had ever frequented her bakery before. Robots don't have much need for cake.

"Can I help you?" Chirri purred. "Are you here to deliver an order?"

With a strange chorus of squeaks, the robot turned away from the commitment ceremony cake it had been eyeing and approached Chirri at the counter. "Yes," it said. "I would like to order one of those." It pointed back at the six-tiered, pink-frosted cake covered in Hegulan flowers and dusted with Aldebaran sugar crystals.

Chirri had never sold a cake that large before.

"Can we—I mean, can I take that one?" The robot's arm

squeaked as it lowered from pointing at the cake. It must need oiling.

"Unfortunately, that cake is for display only," Chirri admitted. She'd baked it with a mix of preservatives that meant it would be all but inedible but that had kept it beautiful for months. For a moment, she wondered whether it would really be wrong to sell an inedible cake to a robot that couldn't eat it... Perhaps the robot only wanted to look at it? But her conscience got the better of her. "Tell me exactly how you want your cake, and I can make you one to order."

The robot was surprisingly indecisive for a creature with a computer for a brain—first it wanted red frosting, then blue, and finally settled on green. It asked whether the cake could be made any bigger, and Chirri had to insist that she couldn't make it more than eight tiers high without compromising its structural integrity. Finally, she asked where the robot would like the cake to be delivered, and the robot said, "Do you know the All Alien Cafe?"

"Of course," Chirri said.

"Around the corner from there, two doors into the residential quarter." The robot paid for the cake and left Chirri to her baking and musing.

Perhaps the robot was throwing a party. Perhaps the robot was in love with an organic life form and wanted to make a grand gesture. As Chirri mixed the batter, she let her curiosity run away with her, imagining all kinds of scenarios. *Perhaps the cake was part of a scientific experiment. Perhaps performance art.* As she decorated the cake, sprinkling on the Aldebaran sugar and carefully placing each Hegulan rosette, Chirri hoped that she'd see what the cake was for when she delivered it.

However, Chirri was disappointed the next day when she floated the cake on an anti-grav trolley to the robot's door. The door slid partway opened, and amidst much squeaking, the robot's domed head peaked out, but when the robot saw her, it only opened the door far enough to let the cake in before thanking Chirri and closing the door in her felinid face. Her triangular ears flattened in disappointment, and she turned to go, telling herself that some mysteries were never meant to be understood.

Then she remembered the cake-topper in her pocket. The robot had requested a custom cake-topper molded out of caramel and chocolate in the shape of swirling gas planet with rings. She'd meant to affix it to the top of the cake at the last moment, keeping it safe until then.

Chirri knocked again at the robot's door. There was no answer, so she tried the control panel and the door slid open. In its excitement, the robot must have forgotten to lock the controls. Do robots get excited? Chirri realized that it didn't matter, for this was not a robot. It was a mecha.

The dome-headed metal mecha had been abandoned just inside the door, and dozens of tiny purple-furred mouse-like aliens were streaming out of its boxy metal foot, rushing in great excitement toward the cake which had been moved to the middle of the room.

The room itself was filled with knee-high buildings, and skyscrapers the height of Chirri were all around the edges of the room. At first, the tiny purple-furred aliens were too busy to notice the gigantic feline alien who had intruded into their realm—they had a cake the size of a mansion! Families laid out picnics beside it, and couples danced to music played by a tiny rock band that had set up their instruments on the first tier as if it were a stage.

Chirri's feline eyes grew wide at the mesmerizing sight. Finally she cleared her throat, and when hundreds of tiny eyes turned to her, she held out the chocolate and caramel planet. One of the mice wearing a tiny uniform squeaked and pointed at the top of the cake. Chirri couldn't understand the mousie-alien's tiny voice, but she placed the ringed planet on top of the cake and all the little aliens in the room broke out in applause. Chirri wondered if chocolate planet was a representation of their homeworld.

Then the uniformed mouse scowled and pointed at the door. Chirri bobbed her head and backed away. Before the door slid shut, she said to the room, "Please, come buy another cake from me any time."

18

GALAXY SHAKER AND THE CELESTIAL RAINBOW DRAGON

STAR SHAKER'S scales glittered and shone with rainbow colors under the spotlights. Her barbed tail swayed, and she flapped her tiny vestigial wings as she sang into the mic. With the backdrop of stars behind her, she looked like a mythical creature—a celestial rainbow dragon—not merely a pop-star reptilian alien with a good stage crew.

The crowd roared and cheered in their myriad voices. All kinds of aliens had turned out for Star Shaker's show. They filled the entire atmo-dome, probably doubling the mass of the tiny asteroid that had been hollowed out into a space amphitheater. Star Shaker should have been thrilled, but she'd started to feel like the audience was her enemy—an enemy of a thousand distant faces, none of them real to her, and each of them expecting her to be the perfect artifact they'd seen on their holo-screens and mind-feeds.

As Star Shaker's keening alto rose to a warbling soprano, she raked her hide with the claws of her free hand, shedding rainbow scales like a cloud of petals. A perfectly timed puff of wind blew the floating scales out over the crowd where hands and paws and talons of all sorts reached and jumped to grab the shimmery souvenirs—little pieces of Star Shaker they could take home and treasure.

At the end of the song, Star Shaker bowed deeply, taking a moment's breath before launching into another song. During the relative quiet—those few seconds when the crowd hushed, waiting to hear which song she'd sing next—Star Shaker heard her Robo-weiler guards growling at the side of the stage.

Several performances ago, an antlered alien had broken onto the stage and nearly mauled her, all the while professing undying fandom. So, Star Shaker faltered at the warning sound of her Robo-weilers, but when she looked over, all she saw was a small mammalian alien girl scrabbling for more of the shed scales where some had fallen on the edge of the stage.

The alien girl had long spikes on her back like an echidna or porcupine, and she had decorated them with the little pieces of rainbow. She shimmered like a miniature Star Shaker. Or maybe more like a disco ball. Either way, she was adorable and warmed Star Shaker's cold-blooded and weary heart.

Star Shaker waved her Robo-weiler guards back and came over to kneel down beside the spiky alien child. "What's your name?" she asked and then held the mic out to her.

"Galaxy Shaker!" the child squeaked. "And I'm going to be just like you some day!"

From nearby in the crowd, a larger spiky-backed alien called out, "Her name's Qara, and she knows all the words to every one of your songs."

"Is that so?" Star Shaker asked.

The child nodded her pointy brown-furred snout.

"Would you like to sing with me?"

Galaxy Shaker was fairly vibrating with excitement and didn't even wait for Star Shaker before bursting into a squeaky rendition of the opening words to her most popular song. Star Shaker usually saved it for the finale, but it wouldn't hurt to mix things up.

It turned out that Galaxy Shaker knew all the dance moves too; though they looked different performed by a little spiky ball than by a sinuous reptile with a long tail and wings. Galaxy Shaker danced and sang beside her hero, not missing a beat. The crowd roared like they never had before, even though Galaxy Shaker's squeaky chirps drowned out Star Shaker's smoothly undulating vibrato. It was far from a perfect performance, but it overflowed with heart.

When the song ended, Galaxy Shaker wrapped her furry arms around Star Shaker's scaly knees in a tight hug. Star Shaker grinned down at the fuzzy little ball of spikes, showing off her sharp teeth and forked tongue. She looked fierce, but she felt happy.

Star Shaker leaned down and whisper-hissed into the girl's ear, "You can sing with me any time," before standing back up and yelling into the mic, "A huge round of applause, please, for the first ever performance of GALAXY SHAKER!"

The spiky-backed little girl might have to work up to galaxies, but the asteroid shook with applause.

19

AN ALDEBARAN SUGAR COOKIE FOR STAR SHAKER

THE ASTEROID AMPHITHEATER rocked with applause as the suspended final note of Star Shaker's encore vibrated the atmo-bubble over everyone's heads. The reptilian pop-star bowed and spotlights shone off of her rainbow-colored scales, making her glitter like the stars all around.

Chirri had loved Star Shaker's music since she was a little kitten. Once, she'd even shaved off her fur and drawn little Vs all over her naked skin, hoping they'd make her look like she had scales. It had looked awful, but she'd been too young to care. All she knew was that it had made her feel closer to her hero.

Everything felt right when Chirri listened to Star Shaker's golden throated singing.

The applause died down, and the other fans—all sorts of aliens, from the fuzzy to the feathered, antlered, or scaly like Star Shaker herself—began leaving their seats, heading to the airlocks at the back of the atmo-dome. But Chirri didn't want it to be over. She stayed in her seat, clutching her bag of supplies —snacks, water, vid-com—hoping to catch one more glimpse of Star Shaker.

Of course, it was the fleet of Roboweiler guards who cleared the stage. It was silly to think Star Shaker would come back out, but Chirri couldn't let go of the feeling she'd had while watching her hero, dancing so close, singing in the same air— real sound waves from Star Shaker's silver forked tongue directly to Chirri's eager pointed ears.

Reluctantly, Chirri stood and started edging her way back through the rows of seats, each pawstep taking her farther away from those perfect moments during the concert. She sighed, accepting that the magic had melted away, and it was time to return to her normal life.

Then Chirri saw her: Star Shaker's scales were simply silver-gray without the stage lights, and she was small—a full head shorter than Chirri. But it was her. Alive and real and strutting toward Chirri with a Roboweiler on either side of her. The Roboweilers' mechanical red eyes glowed, menacingly.

Chirri stumbled backward, nearly falling over a seat and tangling her hindpaws in her long tail. When she recovered herself, she could feel that her fur had fluffed out. There were only a few seconds until Star Shaker would pass her on the way to the airlocks, and there would only be a moment then—but there would be a moment. What could Chirri say to her hero in a moment?

Chirri remembered the snacks in her bag—she was a baker and had brought some of her signature Aldebaran sugar cookies. It was stupid... but maybe she could give Starshaker a cookie. Something she'd made for someone who'd made so much for her... Because Star Shaker's music always felt like it was made only for her. She knew it sounded that way to everyone... That was Star Shaker's appeal; she was a reptilian alien, but her heart could have been anything—fuzzy, feathered, photosynthetic—she spoke to them all.

But it didn't matter. Chirri wanted to give her hero something, as a kind of thank you. She dug one of the cookies out of her bag; it was star-shaped and glittered with grains of Alde-baran sugar. Chirri had made the batch especially for this concert. She'd been so excited. And it had been everything she dreamed.

Chirri held out the cookie. Her eyes locked with her hero's, and the small reptilian alien said, "What is this felinoid doing here? I thought you guys cleared this place out."

The Roboweiler to the right snarled and advanced, prob-ably just to warn Chirri to keep her distance from the pop-star, but its mechanical teeth startled Chirri so much that she tripped all the way over the seat this time. She landed splayed on the asteroid amphitheater's floor, ears askew, tail crimped beneath her, and star cookie smashed.

By the time Chirri dusted herself off, Star Shaker and the Roboweilers were well past her. The moment was gone. The moment had been horrible. Chirri relived it—seeing herself over and over again, tripping awkwardly, all dignity lost in front of the one being she most admired.

Chirri's ears flattened and her whiskers shivered. She looked down at the crumbles of sugar cookie in her paw. Maybe she wouldn't bake that recipe again for a while.

In fact, she didn't think she would listen to Star Shaker's music for a while either. At least, until the memory of this night faded. Because she needed that moment to go away, and she couldn't imagine hearing Star Shaker's voice without thinking about it.

The stars still stretched out all around the asteroid amphitheater, but for Chirri, the world had become much smaller, and nothing sounded right. At all.

20

QUEEN DORIPAULI AND THE SPROUTLINGS

SLOANEE'S SLICK, sticky amphibioid fingers wrapped around one of Queen Doripauli's slender twigs. The queen's sea-green fronds uncurled, caressing the richer green skin of her amphibioid lover. Doripauli's yellow daisy-like petals brushed ever-so-lightly against Sloanee's face, and the froggy alien's bulbous eyes closed blissfully.

How could Sloanee give this up? She had loved Queen Doripauli since she'd first set eyes on the photosynthetic floral alien. Her eyes were pink roses; her mouths were blue irises; she was a living bouquet—color and splendor and everything that was right with a universe filled with infinite diversity.

And wonder of wonders, Doripauli loved Sloanee back. Perhaps... Perhaps Doripauli would forgive her.

The queen rose from her repose in the glistening green arms of her beloved. Doripauli's root-like appendages stretched out from her core, carrying her in a rolling gait like a tumbleweed to the computer console at the helm of her royal space cruiser.

"Come back to bed," Sloanee chirruped, hoping to forestall the inevitable conflict. But she knew Queen Doripauli had already made her choices—her plans were in action. Sloanee had no choice but to live with it or follow her conscience.

Sloanee hated her conscience for this.

"It's time to light the fire." Doripauli's voice twinkled like a hundred bells as she spoke from all her blue flowers. "Nothing you need worry about. I'll come back soon."

The queen believed Sloanee didn't care about her political affairs. Sloanee was an alien, an outsider, a safe haven for the queen to escape the pressures of ruling an entire solar system. And at first, that had been true.

What did an amphibioid care for the political concerns of sentient flowers? But Queen Doripauli was about to cross a line that Sloanee could not stand by and watch without action: she was going to set the firelands alight, burning an entire generation of sproutlings.

Sloanee's own people were not overly sentimental about their own young during their early phases of life. Until they'd passed through the taddywog and polipolly stages, their amphibioid brains were rudimentary, barely capable of avoiding pain and seeking food. But once they reached sentience? Sentience must be respected.

Sloanee rose from the bed as well, pulled on her clothes, and removed the metal wand hidden in her pocket. She'd refused the wand the first several times Doripauli's viceroy had pressed it on her. If only she'd turned the viceroy in as a traitor and member of the rebellion that very first time, Sloanee wouldn't be in this situation now... But she had tried so hard to stay uninvolved. So hard. And then Doripauli had brought her for a stroll in one of the nursery green houses...

The amphibioid and floral alien had rambled, side by side, brushing against each other, lost in the romance of each other's company. The very air had sung in praise of their love —at least, that's how it had felt, until Sloanee had realized the twinkling chorus of bells was singing words—she could only make out a few: "Our Queen", "our love", "your royal consort."

It hadn't been romance in the air at all; it had been the sessile plants, growing, rooted in the ground, in rows around them. The sproutlings were sentient, before they ever pulled their roots from the ground.

It was unconscionable to burn down whole fields of them, simply because they'd grown from wild seeds, lost on the wind and settled in the rich soil of the firelands.

Sloanee pressed the red trigger on the metal wand, and a bubble of shimmery force field engulfed Queen Doripauli.

"I can't let you burn the sproutlings," Sloanee croaked. "Give them this continent and let them be."

Queen Doripauli's pink-petaled eyes blinked in surprise, and her sea-green fronds vibrated, singing like outraged violins, "Let me!? This is not your concern. Put down that wand and release me."

"Will you let the sproutlings live?"

"We need the firelands on this planet; Prime World is over-crowded." Doripauli's leaves and fronds shivered and shook with anger. "How dare you make me explain this to you!"

"How dare I confront you?" Sloanee croaked. "How dare I have an opinion?"

"How dare you entrap me!" Doripauli's vines and branches stretched and pressed against the shimmery surface of the force field, but her delicate appendages were no match for quantum space folding.

"Do you love me?" Sloanee asked. A tear formed in the corner of her bulging eyes. "Promise me only that you'll talk to me; let me explain why you can't do this."

"'Can't' is not a word you say to a queen." Doripauli turned her pink-petaled eyes, each and every one of them, away from Sloanee. She refused to even look at the amphibioid alien now that Sloanee had crossed her.

While they argued, Sloanee knew the rebellion, led by the viceroy, was uprooting the sessile sproutlings early, arming them, and expanding the rebellion's numbers. By the time this was over, Queen Doripauli's domain, her entire solar system, would be deep in the throes of a civil war.

It was not Sloanee's war. Sloanee had only one reason to be here. Or maybe... none at all.

"Do you love me?" Sloanee croaked.

"Free me!" Queen Doripauli commanded. Her anger shook her branches so badly, leaves fell from her and cluttered the bottom of the force bubble in a pile.

She was no longer a lover. Only a queen.

The heartbroken amphibioid lowered the metal wand, but she left the queen in her force bubble. The viceroy had promised Sloanee a one-man shuttle and enough time to escape the solar system in return for her cooperation. Even in the middle of a civil war, Sloanee didn't think the queen would make her escape easy. Sloanee would be on the run for a long time.

She would be broken hearted even longer.

21

A SENSE OF CLARITY

HE WAS the kind of guy who would give a fake name. Clarity could tell by the way he tentatively tried sitting at three different tables before settling down on a seat at the bar; also, the way his bulgy, protuberant eyes kept glancing around nervously; and, finally, the way he glared piercingly at his mottled green, slumped reflection in the mirror behind the bar before answering her question.

"So, what's your name?" she asked.

"Uh... Stanley," he answered, sure enough.

There was no way that an amphibioid alien like this guy had a classic terran name like Stanley. But Clarity had been tending bar for long enough at the All Alien Cafe on Crossroads Station—three weeks now!—to know better than to give a customer any trouble. It just ate into her tip.

"What's your drink, Stanley?" she asked, and, while she concocted the vile gray mixture of alcohols he ordered, Clarity ran through all the other questions she could ask him in her mind. *Where are you from? What brings you to Crossroads Station? Why haven't I seen your species here before?* But he'd already given a fake name, so he'd probably lie to any of them. Still,

Clarity got better tips when she engaged the customers in conversation, so she handed his drink over with a winning smile and said, "I flew here on a cargo ship three weeks ago. It was my birthday present to myself for my eighteenth birthday."

"Happy birthday," Stanley said, lifting his drink to her. He held the glass with his bulgy fingertips hooked over the rim, dipping into the smoky liquid. *Was he drinking it that way? Absorbing it through his skin?* Clarity wasn't sure.

"Thanks," Clarity said. "It seemed like time to get off my native rock. More than time. I mean, I'd only ever met one non-human there! It's such a backwards planet." Clarity babbled for a while about all the aliens she'd met since moving to Cross-roads Station—avian aliens with multi-hued feathers, bushy furred canine aliens, myrmecoid aliens with gleaming exoskeletons and n-jointed legs, among many others.

Stanley didn't say much, but his posture grew easier as his drink slowly and mysteriously disappeared. His pastel green skin took on a glistening sheen, and his oval eyes stopped flit-ting nervously from side to side at the top of his wide face. Instead, he stared at Clarity in a way she found attentive and encouraging. So, she kept on babbling.

By the time Stanley ordered a second drink, Clarity found herself confiding in him about the little crush she had on her boss and how she was looking for a new roommate behind her current roommate's back. The affordable rooms on Crossroads Station were simply too small to share with a complete slob.

Stanley stayed at the bar, ordering drinks and listening to Clarity talk about her life until closing time. She felt like they were old friends, but she knew she might not see him again. A lot of customers passed through the All Alien Cafe once and never returned. That's the way with bars on interstellar travel hubs. Or so Clarity had been told by her boss.

So, it was with some surprise that Clarity saw Stanley slump his way up to the bar the following evening.

"Welcome back, Stan," she said. "Same drink?"

Stanley nodded and hopped up onto the barstool. He was a short guy, probably the same height as Clarity or maybe an inch or two shorter. Of course, Clarity had no way of knowing whether that made him tall or short for his own species. "Have you noticed how much heights vary among different aliens?" Clarity asked, handing over the cloudy drink.

The oval slits of Stanley's eyes narrowed even further, and Clarity realized he might think she was about to turn the conversation toward him. "I mean, take the Heffen over there," she said, quickly redirecting to a table of red-furred canine aliens in the corner. "They're so tall."

Stanley turned to look at the Heffen, and when he turned back, he said, "They seem *human* height to me. On average, anyway." He hooked his fingers into his drink, and the level of the liquid began slowly lowering. "Most of the aliens on a human space station tend to fall within average human ranges, otherwise it can be quite uncomfortable."

Clarity was intrigued. "Have you been to non-human space stations?" she asked, forgetting her caution. But, then, maybe he wouldn't mind having the conversation turn toward him, if she could keep it theoretical enough. "I mean, are there any? Do you know what they're like?"

Stanley eyed the young barmaid carefully, but, in the end, her naive enthusiasm must have won him over. "Have you met any Lintar?" he asked.

Clarity shook her head.

"They're icthyoids," Stanley said, "with delicate fluttering fins. If you'd ever met one, it would have been wearing a breathing helmet and floating. They have swim bladders, you see, and in human atmospheres, well, they can pretty much fly."

Clarity grinned. "And they have their own space stations?"

"Sure," Stanley said. "The Lintar Oligarchy reigned over

this arm of the galaxy long before humans got here." He told her about their spherical space stations—gravity-free and filled with liquid.

"Wow," Clarity breathed. "What else have you seen? Oh, I know! Do you know anything about those bush-like aliens? The ones with all the flowers and leaves that roll around like tumbleweeds?" She'd seen a few tumble their way past the bar earlier—all emerald leaves, pink daisies, blue roses, and mint-green curly fronds. They were among the most beautiful things she'd ever seen, like living bouquets.

The moment Clarity mentioned the plant aliens, though, Stanley's narrow shoulders hunched, and the smooth mottled green skin between his bulgy eyes creased. "I should go," he said, hopping off the bar stool.

"I'm sorry," Clarity said. "You don't have to go. I've got stuff to do in the stockroom anyway." She got out of his way, and when she peeked back from the stockroom a few minutes later, Stanley was still at the bar, frowning at his drink and fiddling his bulbous fingertips in it, playing with the ripples he could make on the surface.

She didn't think he'd be leaving a tip for her today. Still, she wanted to go talk to him. He'd been more real with her than any of the other aliens she'd met on Crossroads Station these last few weeks. Possibly because he didn't have anyone else here either. At least, it seemed that way. And she was worried about him.

When he got up to leave for real, Clarity came over, leaned way over the bar, and said in a low voice, "If you need to talk, I get off in an hour."

Stanley's bulbous eyes goggled in a way Clarity didn't understand, so she just shrugged and said, "You seem like you need a friend. If not, don't worry about it."

But an hour later, Stanley was waiting for her.

The human and froggy-alien wandered through the

merchant quarter of Crossroads Station, commenting on the doodads and tchotchkes for sale. It was pleasant, and Clarity would have loved to think she was building a real friendship with Stanley, but behind it all, he seemed like he was drowning in a deep well of sadness. Finally, Clarity couldn't take it any longer and said, "So, the flower aliens. You didn't like it much when I mentioned them earlier."

If Stanley had had fur, it would have bristled. Instead, his mottled splotches stretched and distorted as his smooth, nearly glistening skin wrinkled. "I don't like it much now either."

Clarity waited, pointedly.

Finally, Stanley conceded, "But you're right. I need to talk. I need to figure out what to do." He looked around nervously. "But not here. Do you have a place?"

Clarity tried to work out in her head whether her room-mate would be home or not. She wasn't sure. "What about your place?"

"Don't have one," Stanley said.

"What, you mean you've just been roaming around the station with nowhere to stay for the last few days?"

Stanley shrugged his skinny arms.

"Where do you sleep?"

"Behind the anti-grav generator in the playground in the refugee quarter."

Crossroads Station generated natural gravity with centripetal forces, since it was a rotating wheel station. However, anti-grav generators that created bubbles of low- or zero-gee were popular playground structures. Clarity had seen the Heffen puppies in the refugee quarter floating and playing tag in the altered-gee bubbles before. She'd also seen the anti-grav generator, and she couldn't imagine sleeping behind it was comfortable.

"Come on," Clarity said. "We'll go to my place."

Clarity's place was a studio—the smallest and cheapest size

of quarters available on the station. Her roommate was an insectoid alien with mechanical wings—kind of amazing, kind of creepy—but Lee-a-lei wasn't home, thank goodness. So, Clarity locked the door and shoved as much of Lee-a-lei's junk off of the small couch as she needed to make space for Stanley.

Clarity perched on the corner of the coffee table. Actually, their only table. But it was short, so she thought of it as a coffee table.

"Tell me about the flower aliens," she said.

Stanley got a faraway look in his bulbous eyes and croaked out the words, "I loved one of them. She was perfect." He said the next word like it was a holy sacrament, "Doripauli." It must have been his beloved's name.

"Didn't go well?" Clarity asked. She didn't have a lot of experience with relationships. She'd had a girlfriend for a few weeks and a boyfriend or two before that. But it had all just been holding hands, passing notes in class, and then being heartbroken when she realized that no one on her backwards planet understood why she wanted to leave.

Now she was here, and she'd seen that relationships could cross all kinds of boundaries—not just gender but species— and it was all kind of intimidating. She had no idea what she wanted anymore.

As Stanley talked about Doripauli though, Clarity started to get an idea: the love story he told of an amphibioid and a photosynthetic floral alien was the stuff of fairy tales. He'd loved Doripauli with his whole heart, every fiber of his being. When her bell-like flowers had chimed his name, it had been enough to send shivers all over his slimy green skin.

Clarity wondered what that name had been—clearly not Stanley.

Some day, Clarity hoped to be in love like Stanley was. Or loved by someone like Stanley. Someone who could spend hours describing her human body the way that he described every one of Doripauli's flowers—the blue light-sensitive ones she used to see; the yellow petaled ones that could taste his skin when they touched; and the green fronds that vibrated, singing like violin strings to form her ethereal voice.

Clarity had no idea how long Stanley might have gone on, rhapsodizing about the wonders of Doripauli, if her roommate hadn't come home. Lee-a-lei beat on the locked door for a while until Clarity let the cyborg butterfly alien in.

Lee-a-lei stomped around, rearranging her junk until she found the jetpack component for her mechanical wings. "Going asteroid hopping," she fluted with her long curled proboscis. "Back tomorrow." She was far more noisy and abrupt than Clarity would have ever pictured a month ago if asked to imagine a butterfly-like alien.

The door slammed behind Lee-a-lei, and Clarity immediately turned back to Stanley. "All right," she said, "I get the love part. But what happened?"

"Political differences," Stanley mumbled, his bulbous eyes clouding.

"Seriously?" That had to be the worst end Clarity had ever heard to a fairy tale.

Something in her tone caught Stanley's attention, because his eyes snapped back into focus on her. He stared at her for a while, measuring her with those giant liquid eyes. She must have measured up, because he said, "Doripauli's world is over crowded. The solution? They decided to burn an entire generation of sproutlings. I helped a small band of rebels free the sproutlings from the firelands before it was too late. Now her world is plunged into the depths of a civil war, and Doripauli is on the other side."

That was more like it—life and death, generations pitted against each other, war and love torn asunder. It was horrible. But Clarity couldn't help loving it. The universe out here was so big.

Then she looked into Stanley's eyes and saw the depth of his pain—big enough to match the size of his story.

"I don't know what to say," Clarity said. "I feel like I should offer you some advice, but I don't even know how to tell my roommate how unhappy I am with her junk all over." Clarity shoved at a pile of indistinct fabric with one foot. She wasn't even sure what it was—it wasn't like Lee-a-lei wore clothes over her exo-skeletal body. "I have no idea what you should do."

To her surprise, Stanley responded, "I know what I need to do. I just don't know if I can do it."

"What is it?" Clarity asked. "Can I help?" She moved off of the edge of the coffee table to perch instead on the corner of the sofa, closer to Stanley. She reached down and took one of his bulbous-fingered green hands in her own. His skin glistened like it would be slimy, but it was just smooth and surprisingly warm. She'd assumed he was cold-blooded from his amphibioid features, but now she wondered if she was wrong.

Stanley squeezed her hand back and said, "Maybe I just need someone to come with me when I do it—otherwise, I'm afraid I'll lose myself completely. Will you come with me? Would you really do that?"

Clarity felt like she'd missed a step and worried that she'd agreed to do more than she was comfortable with. But Stanley looked so hopeful for the first time since she'd met him, and after talking all night, she felt like she knew him deep into his soul. Even if her feelings were only an illusion caused by the excitement of their sudden intimacy, it was still dizzying, and Clarity found herself saying, "Anywhere."

Stanley led Clarity through the refugee quarter of Crossroads Station to the sketchiest, most rundown hole-in-the-wall restaurant she'd ever seen. The dingy paper signs taped to the walls—yes, actual paper—claimed the menu featured fusion cuisine, but didn't say which cuisines they were fusing. Human?

Heffen? Other aliens? All of them together? Clarity was relieved when Stanley led her straight through the empty restaurant to a curtained off room in the back. In there, the walls were plastered with pictures of different alien species, but these were flashing over vid-displays instead of printed on paper.

An antlered alien with a long neck, floppy ears, and wide round feet like an elephant's pushed aside a curtain in the back and came into the room to greet them. Clarity had never seen an alien like this one before. Honestly, it looked like an amalgam of other aliens. Some sort of bizarre chimera.

"You're back," the antlered alien said. "Are you serious this time?"

"I was serious before," Stanley said, reaching subtly and nervously out for Clarity's hand. She let him take it, and he squeezed really tight. "I don't have a choice. I just... needed time to get used to it."

"Have you decided what you want to be?" the antlered alien asked.

"Not yet," Stanley said. "Can we see the menu?"

The antlered alien snorted but then adjusted one of the vid-screens. It began displaying a list of alien features and phenotypes alongside astronomical prices. "I'll give you some privacy." The antlered alien stomped back through the curtain, leaving it swinging.

"What is this place?" Clarity asked.

"The Genie Shop," Stanley said.

"Genie?"

"It's short for Genetic Errant—someone who's had their physical form altered from the genetic form they were born with. Some of it is legal. Some of it isn't. A lot of it is used to... escape legal consequences."

"Why are we here?" Clarity asked. She put her free hand up to the vid-screen and ran her fingers down the different options. Every species she'd seen on Crossroads was listed here, along with many she hadn't seen.

"I told you that I helped the rebels." Stanley turned away from her, but he kept holding her hand. "Their government is looking for me. I'll never be safe in this form. I'm surprised they haven't found me already. I... I should have done this as soon as I got here, but I've already lost so much... It felt like changing my body would mean losing the last I had of myself."

"You really have to do this?" Clarity asked.

Stanley didn't answer, but that was answer enough.

"Okay," she said. "What do you want to be?"

Stanley shrugged, dropping Clarity's hand finally. "I want to be home with Doripauli. Since I can't have that..." He looked back at her, his bulbous eyes again infused with hope. "Will you pick for me? Pick something you'd like."

Clarity looked the choices over. She didn't know what she'd like. She kind of liked Stanley the way he was... but it would be mean to tell him that. If he was trying to hide, the most common species on the station—other than human—was the red-furred canine Heffen.

The antlered alien returned, swishing the curtain aside, and asked, "Have you decided?"

Clarity started to answer, but Stanley said in a rush: "Don't tell me. Let it be a surprise."

"Okay," Clarity said. Then looking to the antlered alien, "Yes, we've decided."

The antlered alien looked back and forth between the human and amphibioid before rolling his eyes, sighing exasperatedly, and saying, "Fine, we can get you started before she tells us what we're turning you into. But *no refunds.*"

Stanley agreed amiably, almost hopping with excitement now that the big decision was out of his hands.

"If you don't like it, too bad," the antlered alien snarled before leading Stanley back behind the curtain. They were gone for several minutes, and then the antlered alien returned alone. "So what are we making Stanley into?"

"Heffen," Clarity said.

"Male or female?"

"Oh, uh, male, I guess."

"So, a gender-flip too," the antlered alien muttered, typing information into the nearest vid-screen.

Clarity started to object, but then she realized that she'd had nothing to base Stanley's gender on other than a typically masculine human name—a name she now realized that she might have misheard. Besides, a gender-flip might be good for helping Stanley elude the flower alien government. "Does Stanley have a gender preference on record?" Clarity asked, wanting to be sure.

"We've discussed all kinds of options. Every species. Every gender. The only preference Stanley's expressed until now is uncertainty."

"Then, yes, male Heffen."

"Okay," the antlered alien said. "It'll take about three weeks. You can go now." Those final words didn't sound like a suggestion. More like an order to get out.

So Clarity did.

She went home to her cramped quarters. Dazed and bereft. She'd spent days making friends with Stanley, only to realize that the person she'd made friends with was on the edge of disappearing. She'd left an amphibioid alien at the Genie Shop, and eventually a Heffen would emerge. And that Heffen had gone to such trouble to rid himself of his past that he was unlikely to ever seek out Clarity again.

Stanley was gone.

Nonetheless, after three weeks passed, Clarity started watching each new Heffen who came into The All Alien Cafe closely, looking for signs of Stanley's slumped posture or soulful eyes. She found nothing. And after a few days, she stopped looking. She also stopped making small talk with the customers. Sure, it got her bigger tips, but it was too hard—feeling that flicker of potential friendship followed by the hardening in her heart as she protected herself. It was easier to keep a distance.

Then a red-furred, perky-eared, bright-eyed Heffen with a swishing tail—as little like Stanley as a customer could be—stopped her after she poured him his drink. He laid a paw on her hand and said, "Hey, aren't you going to ask me my name?"

"What's your name?" Clarity asked mechanically, but as she looked up at the Heffen—far taller than her—she felt a dizzying sensation, like the eyes she was looking into should have been lower and larger. She'd never seen these small, sparkly eyes before, and yet she felt like she could fall into them. They were the eyes of an old friend.

Or at least, a friend.

"I don't have a name yet," the Heffen answered. "I need a new one. Would you pick it for me?"

22

———

WAKING UP IN THE GENIE SHOP

Sloanee opened her eyes and felt her heart racing. What was she doing? Lying down? She was on the lam. She should be running or hiding. Nowhere was safe from the royal guards pursuing her. Queen Doripauli and her army of photosynthetic tumbleweed-like aliens would stop at nothing to catch and punish the amphibioid who had betrayed them.

Betrayed her.

Sloanee shook her head, trying to keep memories of the beautiful floral queen from overwhelming her. Instead, she found herself dizzy and confused; she was having trouble understanding her own body. Sloanee put a hand to her face, but the hand wasn't green and smooth; it was a paw covered in red fur. And her face was wrong: instead of flat and wide, it was long and pointed. She felt her head with her paws and found large triangular ears and a long muzzle. All of it furry.

"You're disoriented," a voice cooed. An avian figure with white feathers and a long graceful neck leaned over Sloanee, offered a wing-like arm, and helped the confused creature up.

"This is the Genie Shop," the white-feathered avian cawed. "You've been here for three weeks. You came to us as a female amphibioid and paid us to change you into a male canid. You're a Heffen now, one of the most common species here on Crossroads Station. So, you'll be in good company."

"Drastic gene therapy," Sloanee croaked. Except, in her new body—his new body—it came out more like a bark. Geez, Sloanee realized, that probably shouldn't even be her—his—name any more.

On the bright side, Sloanee was well hidden from Queen Doripauli's royal guards. They would be looking for a green froggy alien; not this red-furred fox. Sloanee supposed that had been the idea. "Why can't I remember any of this?"

The avian cawed, "The gene treatments interfere with short term memory transfer. Your last day or so before the transition is going to be fuzzy or maybe entirely gone."

"Right," Sloanee barked. A fresh start. That was exactly what she needed. *He needed.* She also needed to start thinking of herself—himself—as a male Heffen. He felt so lost... "What do I do now?"

"I'm sure I don't know," the avian cawed. Perhaps the white-feathered avian could see how lost Sloanee felt, because it took pity and added, "I did hear that you came here with a human girl. A bartender at the All Alien Cafe. If you trusted her to bring you here, then maybe she's somewhere to start."

"Start?"

"Start figuring out your new life," the avian cawed.

"Trusted her?"

The avian bobbed its head several times. "You really are lost. Look, we have a strict privacy policy. No one who works at the Genie Shop will ever connect your previous self with your current self. But that human? If you brought her here with you, then you must have trusted her."

Trust. Sloanee had trusted Queen Doripauli, but the queen had turned against her. What did it even mean to trust someone if that trust had not been true?

"Go on," the avian cawed. "Whatever you decide to do, you can't dawdle around here all day. We have other clients to serve, and for obvious reasons, we can't have you crossing paths with any of them."

"Privacy," Sloanee muttered. The word felt funny in her furry muzzle. Her tongue was shorter, and her mouth narrower than she expected. He expected. Dammit. Sloanee would never keep this straight. Clearly, it had been brilliant to change herself into this totally unfamiliar creature; she could live a life free from persecution now. Except, Sloanee couldn't even remember who he was.

"Right, now get out of here." The avian walked Sloanee out through a curtained waiting room, through a dingy abandoned restaurant front, and into the refugee quarter of Crossroads Station. Before abandoning the confused new Heffen, the avian pointed out the way to the All Alien Cafe in the merchant quarter.

Sloanee wandered aimlessly through the station, missing the spring in her step from her froggy legs but enjoying the way his new tail swished behind him. His ears turned, automatically, to hear the voices and conversations all around. There were a lot of other Heffen here, just like the white-feathered avian had said. It would be easy to disappear.

In fact, Sloanee felt like she was about to disappear entirely. All that was left of her were some broken, unbearable memories buried deep inside this new body—a body that had no life or story of his own. Who was he?

In spite of herself, Sloanee found that her paws steered her to the All Alien Cafe. She had nowhere else to go. She sat down on a stool at the bar inside. No one gave her a second glance. A handsome male Heffen was commonplace here.

A pink-skinned primatoid with long head fur served Sloanee a drink, and the new Heffen watched her working the bar. This was the human girl that the avian had mentioned.

Sloanee remembered meeting her before. Her name was Clarity, and she'd seemed kind. The last thing Sloanee could remember before waking up in the Genie Shop was Clarity serving a drink and asking, "What's your name?"

Whatever had happened after that was gone. Except for a feeling of warmth. Sloanee felt more rooted in herself around this human.

On an impulse, Sloanee reached out a red-furred paw and placed it on the human's hand. "Aren't you going to ask me my name?" Sloanee asked.

The human looked surprised. "What's your name?" As she stared up into the red-furred canid's eyes, there was a glimmer of recognition, even though she could never have seen Sloanee in this body before.

Sloanee felt a rush of relief, as if being recognized by this human she hardly knew meant that she wouldn't lose herself entirely in this new form. "I don't have a name yet," Sloanee said. "I need a new one." With a deep breath, Sloanee prepared to leave her old self behind and truly become someone new. "Would you pick it for me?"

23

BETWEEN THE BLACK HOLES

THE BINARY BLACK hole sucked all the glittering starlight around into its twin maws. It stared at the viewscreen like two dark eyes, windows into the void.

"You've got to be kidding," Clarity said, twisting her dyed-green hair nervously around her fingers. "We can't fly between those things."

The pilot of the small starhopper, a red-furred canid, stared right back at the pair of black holes, orbiting each other in a mad, spiraling dance that would end in eventual merging. Centuries from now. "Dead serious," he said, triangular ears laying back flat against his head.

The Heffen and human sat in their pilot and co-pilot seats in a starhopper perched on the edge of star-crushing nothingness. The walls of their ship felt very thin with that binary black hole filling the viewscreen.

"Come on, Iroh," Clarity said to the Heffen. "There has to be a better option—turn yourself in to the authorities on Crossroads Station and ask for asylum—"

Iroh shook his head, refusing to even meet his human friend's eyes.

"—okay, or go to the Genie Shop again and get another genetic mutation?" Clarity was twisting her dyed-green hair nearly hard enough to pull it out.

Iroh turned to face Clarity, his muzzle drawn into a serious frown, and said, "And you'll get changed too? Maybe into a reptilian S'rellick? We could both become reptiles. Or do we part ways?"

Clarity's brow creased. "Good point." She didn't want to change herself into a different species... She'd seen how hard that had been for Iroh. The red-furred canid had been a bulgy-eyed amphibioid when she'd met him. Met her. They'd met only days before the transition from female-frog to male-dog, and by all rights, Iroh shouldn't have shared who he'd been before with anyone. Let alone a random bartender. But changing that much of yourself... It was too hard for Iroh to do it alone.

"Well, we'd be doing it together..." Clarity still didn't want to and was relieved when Iroh shook his head again. "Fine, then," she said, "Face your fears and turn yourself in to the Diasporans."

Iroh barked a harsh laugh. "You've never actually met a Diasporan, have you?"

Considering that the be-flowered tumbleweed-like aliens had been the villains in her life since meeting Iroh, she'd had shockingly little direct contact with them. One or two had come into the All Alien Cafe while she was bartending, before she met Iroh, but that was it. "Well, they're basically sentient flowers. How bad can they be?"

"Heartless," Iroh said. "For one."

"A physiological condition of being plants," Clarity countered.

"Literally and metaphorically." Iroh spoke the words quietly. He'd been in love with a Diasporan once, before he'd aided the sproutling revolution and been placed at the very top of their queen's Most Wanted list. Back when he'd been a sentient frog.

Iroh's eyes dropped from where they'd been locked on the twin black holes, and his voice lowered to a mere rumble: "I can put you into the escape pod, leave you in stasis with a looped distress call, on course for the nearest space station. But I'm flying this starhopper between those black holes." He glanced at her sidewise, not wanting to show the pain in his eyes, but wanting to see what was in hers.

Clarity's eyes were full of tears. Her big red-wolf that had rescued her from the pedestrian life of serving bar, too much in debt to enjoy the exciting space station where she had lived, was offering to say goodbye to her. Forever.

Clarity reached a hand out, and Iroh grasped it desperately with his paws.

"I'm not leaving you," Clarity said. Flying between those black holes looked like a death wish to her, but she would fly into death's crushing embrace with Iroh. She'd fly anywhere with him. She wanted to ask whether he really believed it was safe, but instead, she said simply, "Let's do this."

Iroh's wolfish muzzle split into a grin. A grin bright enough to cancel out two black holes. He didn't say anything. He didn't have to with a grin like that. It said everything for him. Instead, he simply squeezed Clarity's hand before taking his paws back to work the controls.

Irrationally, Clarity tightened the safety belts on her seat. As if safety belts would make a whit of difference if they were grabbed by the event horizon of either black hole. "Fly straight," she said, voice catching with fear.

"I've got this," Iroh said, eyes once again locked on the the viewscreen. Though he shot one glance to the side, to check on her, and added, "I've got you."

Clarity leaned back in her co-pilot's seat and closed her eyes. But with her eyes closed, she imagined she could feel the two black holes pulling at her, grasping at her from either side with their impossibly strong gravity. It was all in her head, but it was too horrible to bear, and she opened her eyes again to watch as the last of the glittering lights shot away off the side of the viewscreen.

All was blackness. With the artificial gravity, they couldn't even feel the speed they were picking up, slingshotting between the black holes, gaining the largest gravity assist available in the universe.

"Pick a direction," Iroh said, still focusing on the controls.

"What?"

"We can go anywhere in the universe. Point in a direction, and we'll go find a galaxy to explore."

Stars began appearing in the distance again. Crystal constellations and entire galaxies glowing brightly on the far side of the binary black hole. They had survived. They were through, and they were flying fast.

A triple-spiral galaxy, glittering with blue and yellow swirls caught Clarity's eye. She wondered what kind of sentient species lived there. What kind of worlds they could find. With a shaking hand, she pointed to it.

24

OF STARWHALS AND SPACESHIPS

A metal behemoth cruised through the nebula, cool and casual, like it didn't care about any of the frolicking younglings and their sing-song radio waves or the older starwhals jockeying for territory, rearranging the ambient dust into moats and walls.

The attitude of the metal creature—the complete nonchalance—intrigued Chlooie, and she followed it on its strangely linear course through the nebula.

Chlooie swam through the empty vacuum of space in a laconic sine wave, examining the metal beast from one side and then the other, back and forth, lazily. It seemed to be in an awful hurry, flying so straight. Everything about it was exotically angular and hard edged.

Chlooie sent out a gentle interrogative radio wave from her spiral cranial horn, and moments later, she was answered with a tingly sensation throughout her blubbery teardrop-shaped body. The sensation startled her, and she jetted away from the metal creature with a blast from her dorsal tube organ.

"Who?"

The question appeared in Chlooie's mind, all jumbled up—

like she couldn't tell if she'd heard it or seen it or remembered it from a long time ago. Still, it made her picture herself: one of the smaller starwhals in her litter, recklessly curious, too old now to play with the younglings but not yet interested in the games of the adults. An outsider.

"Chlooie," she thought back at the voice she'd heard, hoping it would ask her more questions. Hoping it was the voice of the metal beast. Hoping it would play with her.

"Nice to meet you. I'm Arellnor."

Along with the words echoing in her mind, Chlooie saw a completely nonsensical image: a tiny fuzzy creature with a pair of complicated branching horns sprouting from its weirdly round head that topped a body with four utterly aerodynamically useless jointed appendages. It made Chlooie laugh. Her blubbery body shook with the laughter.

"That's not what you look like," Chlooie thought back at Arellnor, all while picturing Arellnor's proper metal body with all its weird straight edges and sharp angles.

Arellnor projected back several confusing images of the antlered body being eaten by the metal body, but Chlooie lost interest in her new friend's body dysphoria and suggested they play a game.

So they raced each other, chased each other, sang and swapped stories. Arellnor was on a long journey and appreciated the company; Chlooie loved that Arellnor would play with her and delighted at the strange images she shared.

"I have to stop here," Arellnor thought when they came to a solar system swarming with other metal creatures. They all swam through space in weirdly straight lines like Arellnor, but otherwise seemed nothing like her. Many of them were far larger than Arellnor, and their shapes varied far more than starwhal shapes did.

None of them answered Chlooie when she pinged them with her radio waves. It was like they were dead inside. Creepy.

Arellnor nosed up against the largest metal creature in the system. Chlooie had never seen anything like it—it was shaped like several concentric rings, connected by spokes, and many of the smaller metal creatures were nosed against it. Was it a different stage in their lifecycle? A mother suckling the younglings?

"Why don't the other metal beasts talk to me?" Chlooie asked.

"They think your voice is static and block it out," Arellnor answered. "I'm going to be busy for a while. Will you wait for me?"

Chlooie pictured a span of time and agreed to return. Truth be told, after such a long flight, she could use a stop for sustenance as well. Chlooie left the brood of metal behemoths to their strange ways and found a tasty gas giant. She skimmed along the planet's frothy surface, sucking up astro-microbes and nutritional minerals through her baleen maw. When her belly was sated, Chlooie dove and surfed in the planet's heavy gravity for a while, just for fun.

When the span of time had passed, she swam her way in lazy spirals toward the metal ring mother, but before she got there, she passed Arellnor flying back in the direction they had come.

"Arellnor!" Chlooie thought. "Shall we race again?" She had energy to burn.

But Arellnor didn't respond.

"We could sing?"

But Arellnor didn't respond.

Chlooie followed her friend, pinging her with radio waves and beseeching her with thoughts, but Arellnor had changed. After feeding at the ring mother's teat, she'd gone dead inside like all the other metal behemoths in this system. All she would do was fly straight and true. No images. No songs. No games. No playing.

No Arellnor.

Chlooie's dorsal tube organ fluttered in a heartbroken sob. Arellnor had outgrown her, just like the other starwhals. She wondered if she should return to her home nebula and try to grow up too.

Then she felt the familiar presence in her mind, but it didn't come from Arellnor. It came from another, different metal monster.

"I'm sorry," the metal monster thought at her. "I wasn't expecting to have to trade ships. This must be a shock for you." Along with the words came the picture of Arellnor's self-image, the strange antlered body, inside of this new metal monster. Somehow, Arellnor's soul had transferred from one metal body to the other. "I needed a little extra cash, so I traded my old ship in for an even older one," Arellnor thought. "But it's still me."

Chlooie swam around this new metal body, examining it from every side: Arellnor was even smaller and more angular now; her metal skin was darker and pockmarked with age. But her voice sounded the same. Her crazy self-image with antlers had stayed the same.

"Will you still travel with me?" Arellnor asked.

Chlooie knew she'd go home eventually, but she had time for a few more adventures with her friend before she grew up. "Yes."

25

HEART OF THE GAS GIANT

THE HEART of the gas giant was the key. Arellnor had traveled from one star system to another; at every stop, she'd traded her vehicle—first her trusty shuttle for a star-hopper, then that for a space mecha-suit and finally back to another shuttle. She'd altered her appearance, buying gene-therapy or cosmetic-sculpting every chance she got. She barely remembered what she'd been originally—some sort of space frog? Today, she was a burly antelope-like alien; her fingers were rough and hard, and antlers rose from her head like spires. None of it had been enough. They were still chasing her.

Arellnor might barely remember herself, but she remembered why they were after her. That was burned into her heart: an image of flowers and branches, the queen of a race of photosynthetic aliens. Doripauli had loved her once, and Arellnor—no matter what else she had become—loved the delicate creature of blossoms and vines still.

But Doripauli had been wrong, and Arellnor had defied her. She had freed the sproutlings. Now with everything left of her empire, Doripauli pursued Arellnor; her centurions would stop at nothing, and Arellnor had but one choice left.

The gas giant's creamy amber clouds swirled beneath the shuttle, and with a final deep breath, Arellnor began the shuttle's descent, hoping the rumors she'd heard were true. This was her only way out.

Wisps of gold streamed past the shuttle's windows, thickening and darkening. Tawny cirrus clouds gave way to puffy cumulous masses. *Would Doripauli's fleet follow her into the gas giant or wait for her to emerge? Did they know why Arellnor was here?* It didn't matter; Arellnor wasn't coming back, and they could never catch her in time.

Lightning flashed in the murky umber clouds, and after its brightness, everything left was dark. The shuttle was too deep now for sunlight to reach it through the thick soupy layers of atmosphere. Soon she would know if she was finally safe or ultimately caught.

Sparkles shimmered in the dark, shining off the edges of the clouds. The sparkles grew and resolved, forming the shape of fins. Eerie gas giant denizens, fish-like and fluid, floating through the clouds in the distance. The shuttle barreled downward, and the shimmery fishes followed it, swarming and flocking. Arellnor should have felt relief—*the rumors were true*—but all she felt was numb.

The radio crackled to life in Arellnor's shuttle, and a voice spoke in chiming tones: "On behalf of her highness Queen Doripauli, we command you to turn yourself over."

Arellnor's resolution faltered—she pictured returning to Doripauli in her current ungulate form; the queen's soft green vines would twine around Arellnor's spear-like antlers; her purple eye-flowers would flutter, and her leaves would brush gently against Arellnor's short brown fur. Except, that wouldn't happen.

Arellnor would be executed. Perhaps without even seeing the queen. Doripauli looked frail and floral, but her heart was as hard as stone.

Her heart. Arellnor nearly laughed at the thought. *How had she ever thought Doripauli had a heart?* Her vines and branches didn't have a circulatory system like Arellnor's. No matter how much Arellnor's outer features had changed—slimy smooth amphibious skin, coarse folds of blubber, or bushy long fur—her heart had always beat the same inside.

Why had she ever loved a fickle flower? And why did it have to be one who was so powerful? Yet Arellnor loved Doripauli still. If she could have gouged out that part of her heart, she would have. Instead, all she could do was hope for escape to a universe where her wounded heart could heal in peace.

The school of gas giant fish spiraled around the shuttle; their bioluminescence sparkling like fireworks. Arellnor heard another voice, but it didn't chime over the radio. Words echoed like a chorus singing inside her antlered head: "*You are here for the portal.*" It was a question and it wasn't. The gas giant fish knew.

"Yes." Arellnor whispered the word to herself inside the shuttle, but that was enough. The school of fish heard her, and they spiraled faster.

"*We don't know where it goes,*" the chorus of fish sang. Their sparkles blurred together as they swam in circles, blending into a single glowing whirlpool of light. "*It leads to a different universe every time.*"

Arellnor didn't care. She would leave behind everything in this universe; she only wished she could leave herself behind too.

Without another moment of hesitation, Arellnor piloted the shuttle into the shimmering whirlpool of light. As the glow engulfed her, she mouthed a silent 'thank you' to the chorus of fish and prepared to discover her life all over again, starting over in an entirely new universe.

26

___

CHRYSALIS PARTY

JADE'S BELLY was full of food from a dozen star systems, but she felt hollow. It was her place, as Moryheim's closest friend, to pour the glass of Khenani-catalyst wine that would begin her friend's change. Having attended dozens of K'shellica chrysalis parties, Jade had thought this time would be no different. It was always hard to say goodbye to her K'shellican friends, but she now realized it was much harder to pour the wine herself.

"It's time," Moryheim urged with her rumbly voice.

Jade looked around the party: a vast picnic spread on the chartreuse grass under Moryheim's chosen tree. All the guests —mostly K'shellican, but a few humans like herself—had turned their faces toward her in expectation. With shaking hands, she picked up the carafe and poured the deep brown liquid, spilling only a little. She handed the glass to Moryheim, who took it with the chubby, green-skinned fingers of her uppermost arms. Moryheim's other arms squeezed herself, wrapping her long caterpillar-like body up in a quadruple hug. Jade wondered if her friend was scared of the change.

When they'd spoken the night before, Moryheim had been excited, not scared. She had tried to sweep Jade up in it:

wondering what her body would be like after her months of metamorphosis.

"My egg-mother had purple flecks in the folds of her wings," Moryheim had said, looking down at her body and gesturing with several arms at the phantom wings of her imagining. Time would make those wings real, but Jade doubted that Moryheim would have time for her anymore when that happened.

The larval stage of the K'shellican life-cycle lasted nearly twenty human years. Plenty of time to make friends and build attachments that felt like they would last forever. However, the adult form was vastly more intelligent, and Jade had yet to meet a K'shellican adult who had time for humans. Their mathematics and philosophy had changed everything from religion to the basics of space travel across a multitude of cultures. They were among the most respected thinkers of any species that humanity had encountered. Jade admired Drogash the Illuminator, Chora the Harmonic, and Ghee Mo more than she could say.

But she also missed who they'd been before their chrysalis parties.

Moryheim drank the catalyst wine. Shudders rippled over her long body, but she rose until she was standing on only her four hindmost limbs. She held her uppermost arms aloft and grabbed the lowest limb of her chosen tree. She swung herself upward. Jade could already see Moryheim's body stiffening.

The other guests danced and sang while Moryheim spun the silk cocoon that would hold her for the next few months. Jade sat as still as a stone, watching the silver strands wind around her friend.

"I'll still be your friend," Moryheim said, almost as if she could read Jade's mind.

Jade couldn't bring herself to say anything—no comforting platitudes, nothing she didn't mean, and certainly none of the bitter recriminations she felt in her heart. Moryheim didn't deserve her bitterness.

"Why do you keep making friends with us?" Moryheim asked. The silk strands covered most of her body now. Soon, her face would disappear beneath a silk so fine it was almost clear.

"I don't know," Jade said. But she wondered. "Maybe it's the thrill of being close to greatness. Maybe I just enjoy the companionship of larval K'shellicans. Or maybe I hope you'll remember my friendship—that something we've shared will affect the super-intelligent being you're about to become."

"That's certainly true." Moryheim continued winding the silk around herself as she spoke. "Much of who I am is due to you."

Jade had her doubts. But she also had hopes. Maybe this time would be different. "Tell you what," she said. "When you emerge from your chrysalis, you'll be far better able to answer your own question than I am."

Moryheim chuckled.

"So, come find me then." Jade looked down at the shadow cast by Moryheim's chrysalis on the ground. She nearly choked on the words, "You tell me the answer." She knew Moryheim wouldn't.

The other guests departed, one by one, until only Jade was left, sitting under the tree beside a silver cocoon nearly twice her size. Moryheim's final question haunted her. Jade wondered if she should leave K'shellica—move back to a human space station and make friends who wouldn't outgrow her.

Then she thought of the first time she'd read an essay by Drogash after his change—the world, life, and meaning itself had never seemed so clear. Chora's symphonies were ecstasy incarnate. And, if Jade did leave K'shellica, the trip to the nearest space station would be months shorter due to Ghee Mo's bent-space portals.

She had known each of them. She had been their friends. Maybe in her small way, she had changed them. They had certainly changed her. Each one of them.

Jade wondered what Moryheim would do when she emerged from her chrysalis with purple-specked wings and hyper intelligence. She got up and laid her hands on the warm silk of Moryheim's chrysalis. "Goodbye, friend," she said. Then she walked away from Moryheim's tree, back to her home in the larval barracks.

27

ONE ALIEN'S WINGS

LEE-A-LEI'S WIDE WINGS FLUTTERED, casting pools of colored light that chased each other across the walls of the robotics laboratory. The harsh fluorescents from the ceiling softened to warm reds, golds, and chips of blue or green as they passed through her translucent wings.

"Are you sure?" asked the roboticist, a human woman named Maradia. As she looked at the beautiful lepidopteran alien, a veritable stained glass window come to life, it was almost impossible to believe that she'd agreed to take this commission. She almost hoped that Lee-a-lei would change her mind and leave Maradia with a month of wasted work and a useless pair of mechanical wings.

Lee-a-lei's mouth parts stirred, and her long proboscis uncurled. The sounds she emitted were half flute, half violin. Yet Maradia could just make out the Solanese words, "I'm sure. If I'd stayed among my own people, I'd have cut them off long ago."

"They're so beautiful," Maradia sighed.

"They're vestigial," Lee-a-lei intoned, holding out a knife with one of her six claw-like hands. "Cut them off."

Reluctantly, Maradia reached out for the knife. Her human fingers brushed against the coarse hairs on Lee-a-lei's claw-hand. A pool of ruddy light fell on the knife blade. Maradia shuddered, but she did her job. She ran the sharp blade along the crease between Lee-a-lei's hard carapace and the soft flesh of her wing.

The blade came away gummy, and the wing crumpled to the floor like a discarded scarf. It twitched once. But Lee-a-lei didn't even flinch, merely stood by patiently while Maradia cut off the second one.

Lee-a-lei stood now before Maradia, strangely diminished. Her body hadn't changed, but the lack of her bounteous wings made it seem to have. Segmented arms and armor-like carapace, dozens of wiggly mouthparts nestled at the base of a long, curled proboscis, and antennae that moved about restlessly above giant multi-faceted domed eyes—that's all she was now. A monster who had been an angel. Maradia could see why Lee-a-lei had chosen to keep her wings so long after puberty while living in human society.

"Are you okay?" Maradia asked.

"I feel... so light!" Lee-a-lei twirled about, stretched out her segmented arms and danced like a nightmare come to life. "If I'd known how good I'd feel without them, I'd have done this years ago."

"You still want the robotic ones, right?"

Lee-a-lei hesitated, antennae rotating, and for a moment Maradia thought she might get stiffed on this job anyway. Then the former-butterfly alien said, "Yes. Let's put them on."

This was the part Maradia was comfortable with: she lifted the pair of robotic wings, constructed from ultra-light alloys, and affixed them to Lee-a-lei's back. Smart wires wormed their way from the base of the mechanical wings into Lee-a-lei's carapace to bond with her nervous system. Little lights along the edges of the metal wings twinkled, showing they were operational.

"So pretty!" Lee-a-lei exclaimed, sounding like a happy orchestra. She flapped her metal gray wings proudly; they were barely a quarter of the size of her old ones.

Maradia looked down at the crumpled organic wings on the floor, still rich with vivid hues. As a roboticist, she was proud of the metal wings she'd made—they were crammed full of clever devices like personal climate-adjusters, gyroscopic balancers, jetpack boosters, and limited anti-grav—but they looked plain and gray in comparison to the ones discarded at her feet.

The metal wings were a common expression of Maradia's skill as a roboticist; Lee-a-lei's organic wings had been a marvel of biology.

"What do you want me to do with these?" Maradia asked, shoving her foot against the folds of colors.

"Whatever you want," Lee-a-lei said. She was busy testing the anti-grav capability of her new wings—hovering lightly over the floor. "This is wonderful!" she exclaimed. "My old wings didn't let me fly at all!"

"I'm glad you like them," Maradia said, wondering if the old wings could be preserved and turned into some sort of cloak. "Come back in a couple weeks so I can give your new wings a tune-up, make sure they've bonded properly with your nervous system, that sort of thing."

Lee-a-lei's expression was hard to read, but her multi-faceted eyes sparkled. She paid double for her new wings, insisting that they were worth it, and left the laboratory an all new butterfly.

Maradia picked up the old wings off of the floor, draped them over her shoulders, and tried to imagine feeling their lovely weight and warmth as a burden.

28

THE PINK AGATE

Clori, a koala-like woman, twisted wires about the pink and white agate in her paws, bending the delicate silver strands carefully with her claws. When she was done, the heart-shaped stone's wavy lines were cradled in a net of silver that she hung from the mosaic of agates—each one collected by one of her adopted children.

Clori wouldn't have expected T'reska to pick a pink agate. The little green-scaled reptilian child was perhaps the least like Clori of all of her children.

Usually, T'reska asked for everything to match her green scales. Yet, when told to pick an agate to represent her in the mosaic, the little lizard girl had picked the pinkest, warmest looking stone of them all.

A warm stone to represent a cold-blooded child.

Clori felt the air move, rustling the long gray fluffs of fur on her large, round ears, and she heard whispered giggles. She looked over to see three little faces peaking at her from around the corner to the bedroom hallway. Three little faces that should have been in bed—Lut's long beaked face, Anno's scruffy red-furred muzzle, and Iko's wide, wide eyes, almost the entirety of her sweet little primatoid face.

"Is it done?" Lut cawed, feathers puffing out.

"Hush!" Anno woofed, trying to shove the other two back into the shadows, as if Clori hadn't already seen them.

"We just want to see it!" Iko squeaked, swinging herself under Anno's blocking arms. She scrambled right up onto Clori's lap, knocking about all the carefully arranged agates that hadn't been wrapped yet.

"You'd better not wake the others," Clori admonished.

"Oh, none of us were sleeping," Anno woofed helpfully.

Clori sighed. She'd been mad to have this many children. Sometimes, her household felt less like a family and more like a zoology experiment. Of course, at one level it was—one child of each of the twelve most common species on Crossroads Station, all raised together, all siblings, all family.

It was an experiment in peace.

Most of the time, it felt like total chaos, and Clori worried that none of them would still speak to each other by the time they were all grown. They'd all hate her for putting them through this, and after raising twelve children, she'd find herself old and alone, none of them by her side.

"This one's mine!" Iko squeaked, delight in her huge eyes, as she pointed to one of the agates already hanging in the mosaic. A gray and blue agate, like an ocean storm, like Iko's wide, wide eyes.

"I know," Clori said. "I remember which agate each of you picked." Some of the kids had taken a long time picking their agates in the lava moon gift shop. It felt like they'd spent longer in the gift shop than watching the actual lunar volcanoes. Would the kids remember the trip fondly? Or would the youngest ones forget it entirely and the older ones remember only the part where Clori had snapped at them about settling into their seats and getting strapped in on the starhopper home? She didn't know.

The bad parts certainly clouded Clori's own memories of the trip, in spite of the bright eclipse moments. There were always moments when their little faces and naive hearts shone through, melting the ice shields that froze over Clori's heart, making her strong and tough enough to survive the daily— hourly—slings and snubs.

"You put my agate next to T'reska's?!" Anno woofed. "Ew! She's not even warm-blooded! I don't know why she's in our family."

Yes. Slings and snubs like that one.

"She's your sister," Clori said, in the calmest, most even tone she could manage. It was hard to even talk to Anno after she said something so ugly. "Go back to bed." She squeezed Iko, who was still on her lap, and then set her down on the floor. The tiny primatoid scurried off, long prehensile tail waving behind her. "All of you," Clori insisted.

Anno grumbled and then whispered with Lut all the way down the hall. The little canine and avian had been thick as thieves lately. On the one paw, Clori was glad to see the two siblings close; on the other paw, they caused so much more trouble together.

They'd used up a month's replicator rations, pretending to run a restaurant for the other kids. Then they'd melted down all of the littler kids' building blocks in the replicator to get enough raw material to print out statues of themselves. Clori didn't even want to know what they'd had in mind for those two statues. It couldn't have been good.

Clori straightened out the remaining agates, and spooled out a length of wire to begin wrapping the next one. Before she could pick though, she saw a little face staring at her from around the corner again. Green and scaly.

Clori held out a fuzzy gray paw and said, "Come on over," to the little reptilian girl.

Green scales, rough and smooth at once, curled up in Clori's lap, pressing down clouds of gray fur and fitting like T'reska had always belonged there.

With a forked tongue, T'reska hissed against Clori's shoulder, "Do you like the heart agate? I picked it to be like you."

"It's beautiful," Clori said, stroking T'reska's scales and rocking the child. "But you were supposed to pick an agate to represent you—not me."

"But that's what I'm like on the inside," T'reska hissed. "Just like you."

Clori closed her eyes, and let the brightness of the moment shine through her. Cold-blooded but warm-hearted. That was her T'reska.

29

THE OLDEST ONE

ANNO WATCHED her mother tuck in each of her siblings to their differently shaped beds. Lut folded his feathered wings into his nest-bed; T'reska stretched out her scaly-green back on her heated bed of rocks; and Iko cradled her primatoid body, swinging lightly, in her hammock. And that was just in this room. The younger ones had been put to bed in their own room an hour ago.

Anno wondered what it would be like to live in a family where everyone was the same species, all of them curled up on flat, round mattresses like her. Sometimes she tilted the mirrors in the bathroom towards each other and watched her reflections fan out—two, four, six... hundreds of red-furred canids smiling back at each other with perked triangular ears and grinning muzzles. All of them happy. She'd liked that. Everyone the same. Everyone getting along.

Instead, Anno was stuck with avian, reptilian, primatoid, felinoid... oh goodness, so many different types of siblings. Practically every species that the Myrmecoid Matrons could genetically tweak to be reproductively viable with Anno's marsupial koala-like mother.

All different. All needing different things. All taking up Mother's time.

Anno waited until she heard Lut whistle-snoring through his beak—he was always the last in the room to fall asleep—and then she crept out of her bed, leaving the blankets in a crumpled pile, and padded softly out of the room. T'reska stared at her with open eyes as Anno passed, but the reptile girl slept that way sometimes. Eyes open. So creepy.

In the hallway, Anno twisted her triangular ears, listening carefully to hear if her mother had gone to bed herself or was still up in the living room. Quiet humming. Anno followed the humming to the living room and peeked around the corner to see her younger brother, Ky the felinoid, purring in their mother's lap as she hummed him a lullaby.

Anno resented that she had to wait her turn to sneak out of bed for a private moment with her own mother. Her triangular ears burned with frustration and impatience as she waited for Mother to shuffle Ky back toward bed. The gray-striped felinoid hissed at Anno as he passed her in the hallway. She merely rolled her eyes at him. It was so cliché for felinoids and canids to not get along. But Ky wasn't old enough to understand that yet.

"What is it, Anno?" Mother asked. The gray koala-like being was always kind, but her voice didn't have the same patience it had held for Ky.

That little cat had used up their mother's patience on himself! Leaving Anno without a gently hummed lullaby of her own... It didn't occur to Anno that her mother might have higher expectations for her, being the oldest.

"Nothing!" Anno woofed, impetuously.

Mother sighed and ran her claws through the long gray fluff of her koala-like ears, like she did every time Anno annoyed her. She'd been doing it a lot lately.

"You clearly don't have time for me," Anno continued, bushy tail swishing. "You never have time for me anymore."

With a sigh, Mother listed all the things they'd done together that day on her claws, and Anno's tail slowed to a sad droop. They had spent the whole day together, but they hadn't spent any of it alone together.

"Now, would you like one last good night hug?" Mother held her fuzzy arms wide, and Anno couldn't resist rushing forward to snuggle in her warmth.

With her head pressed against Mother's belly, Anno felt a squirming that reminded her: even now, she couldn't have her marsupial mother to herself. The family's littlest member had been born two months ago, but it was easy to forget about it... since only Mother had seen the baby before it had hidden inside her pouch to keep developing.

None of the rest of them even knew what species the baby was yet. Anno hoped it was another Heffen like herself. Or even a koala-like Woaoo. Mother claimed that the Myrmecoid Matrons wouldn't do that—they believed in fostering peace between species by forging natal mother-child bonds using their mad-science gene therapies. That meant cross-species relationships.

Still, Anno missed her dim memories of being a baby—just her and Mother; koala and red-wolf, closed circuit. They hadn't needed all the others.

The squirming in Mother's pouch intensified and Anno felt herself kicked by a sibling she hadn't even met yet. "Hey!" she barked. "That's not a great way to introduce yourself to your oldest sister!" She started to growl, and the red fur along the back of her neck prickled out.

Then, to Anno's great surprise, her youngest sibling did pop out an orange-furred knobby head from under the loose blouse covering Mother's gray-furred pouch. Other than the orange colored fur, this new sibling's face looked very little like Anno's.

Or any of her other siblings. He looked more like a giraffe. And in fact, his head rose up and up on a neck that was hilariously long for the size of his head.

The baby made an inarticulate honking sound, and Anno laughed. Though she didn't feel like mocking the new baby. More like showing him off to all of her other siblings.

A keratinous hoof-like hand reached out of Mother's pouch, and Anno wondered what kinds of games that long neck and those hard hands would be good at.

"I'm glad you were here for this," Mother said, giving her oldest child a squeeze.

Anno missed having time alone with her mother, but right now, she couldn't be more excited to have a big crazy family. She couldn't wait to show off this new bizarre baby to them. Tomorrow. For now, Anno's eyes met her mother's, and they both smiled. Red-wolf and koala, closed circuit, encircling a new baby giraffe.

30

ELEPHANTINE DAYDREAM

JEKO STARED out the window at the asteroids and curled her elephantine trunk. She didn't want to be in class with a bunch of dumb Heffen kids and newly sentient robots. The Heffen kids acted like stereotypical canine aliens and kept to their packs, and the robots weren't really kids like her... They showed up one week super-naive and talking all stilted, like computers, and a few weeks later they were smarter than... well... computers, and they graduated out.

For a while, there'd been a S'rellick girl in class, and Jeko had thought it could be cool to make friends with a reptilian alien. (Cool, get it?) But then she went on a hibernation trek to another star system, and Jeko was alone again. The lonely elephant.

A crack and fizzle came from the front of the room, and Jeko looked up to see the Heffen teacher holding a tangled, sparking mess of green wires in his paws. "These are psytrical vines," he said. "They have psychokinetic powers."

"Does that mean they can make chairs float?" one of the Heffen kids barked. "Oh no! I feel it working on me!" The

Heffen boy jumped up on his chair and then threw himself down on the floor, barking with laughter.

"Get back in your seat, Daul," the teacher said with the resignation of having said the same words a million times. "Psytrical vines have the power to carry thoughts—only a short distance, because they're not very powerful, but it's a fascinating experience, and I thought you should all get the chance to try it. So, pair up, and I'll hand out the vines."

The Heffen kids paired up fast, and Jeko ended up with a shiny silver robot partner.

"Oh dear," the teacher said when he came to them. "Psytrical vines only work on organic brains—I have a different project for my robot students." So, he rearranged the pairs until Jeko found herself saddled with Daul, the class clown.

Within seconds of being paired with her, Daul held the pystrical vine up to his wolfish muzzle and barked, "Look at me! I have a long nose like you!"

Jeko wrapped her trunk around herself, wishing she could hide it. Or maybe slap Daul upside the head with it.

"Each partner take an end of your vine," the teacher explained. "Once you each have an end firmly in paw, you should be able to share your thoughts!"

Jeko was a daydreamer, but she was also a rule-follower. So, as much as she didn't want to read Daul's mind, she reluctantly took the other end of his faux trunk with her real one, fully expecting to be hit with an onslaught of disgust and prejudice against her wrinkly gray skin and weirdly prehensile nose.

The green vine crackled electrically in the curl of Jeko's trunk. She didn't see herself at all in Daul's mind. Instead, she found herself swimming in a dizzying array of thoughts—all of them focused on figuring out which Heffen child was most popular today and how to maintain her status—*Daul's status*—amongst them. *How mad could he make the teacher before getting in trouble? If he didn't heckle the teacher would his friends still like him?*

Daul dropped his end of the vine. His eyes were wide. "I didn't know you were so lonely," he said. There was a depth of understanding in his eyes, a true compassion, that Jeko would never have believed before she'd picked up that vine. It made her feel embarrassed to know he'd seen inside her as deeply as she'd seen inside him.

"I hope..." Daul faltered. "I hope you a find a friend."

Jeko's wide ears blushed, and she wondered if he was offering to be her friend. Maybe... Maybe she could be friends with the Heffen kids after all.

Then Daul's eyes clouded with confusion and complication, and Jeko realized that he was calculating whether his own friends would think less of him if he were to hang out with the funny elephant alien. "I mean... a different friend," he blurted and hurried back to the other side of the class.

The rest of the day, Daul darted looks Jeko's way, but she didn't look back at him. She stared out the window at the asteroids, dreaming of when she'd be old enough to pilot a ship and wishing she could learn as fast as the robots.

31

HYPERCRYSTAL WISH

JEKO COILED her long nose around one of the glittering hypercrystals. They weren't really hypercrystals. Just shiny bits of polished, angular glass. Spiky, colorful shapes. But Jeko liked to pretend. She liked to pretend that they were hypercrystals and could grant wishes. She picked up a green star-shaped one and rolled it carefully across her desk with a gentle toss from her prehensile nose.

The robot teacher of Jeko's class said that hypercrystals were just a myth; a quantum physics fairy tale. It wasn't truly possible to slide from one alternate universe to the next simply by applying intellectual willpower to a fragment of broken multi-dimensionality. And even if it were, hypercrystals probably wouldn't look like a noseful of probability dice borrowed from one of the board games at the back of the classroom.

Jeko tossed a purple hypercrystal with twice as many spikes next. It rattled over the desk and bumped the green one. Jeko whispered under her nose, "I wish for friends."

Most of the kids in her class were robots or Heffen, a species of canine alien. Jeko looked more like an elephant. She felt like an outsider with her weird nose-face. The teacher had tried to force her to interact with the other kids, but after a few incidents where the elephant girl burst into tears, the teacher and her parents had decided to back off, giving Jeko a chance to move at her own pace. So far, her own pace involved hiding in the classroom during recess and playing board games alone. But her imagination ran wild. In her mind, she wasn't playing alone—she was voyaging through space, meeting alien races even weirder than herself, and making all kinds of friends.

Jeko wished her parents hadn't decided to settle on Crossroads Space Station. She'd liked it better when they moved from one solar system to the next, never settling. Back then she'd had an excuse for having no friends. Now it felt like her own fault. She swept her nose across the desk in frustration, sweeping all the probability dice back into their cardboard box.

"Are you sure you can't keep playing in the play yard?" woofed a canine voice.

Jeko looked over and saw a pair of her classmates returning to class early: a red-furred Heffen girl named Anno and a green tube-shaped alien with dozens of short arms named Am-lei. Besides Jeko, Am-lei was the strangest alien in the class. She seemed to be some sort of worm. At first, Jeko had hoped their shared weirdness might lead to a kinship between them, but it turned out that Am-lei and Anno had been best friends since long before Jeko moved to Crossroads. Jeko didn't think there was any room in their friendship for her.

"I know jumping through grav bubbles is more fun than stupid board games," Am-lei said, tiny green antennae on her forehead rotating. "But I feel so stiff lately... I just want to sit down."

Jeko felt a burst of excitement as she watched Am-lei bend her long tube-body into a desk only a few empty rows away. Anno skipped to the back of the classroom, fluffy tail swishing behind her, and knelt down to look at the shelf of board games.

Maybe this was just the opportunity Jeko needed. She knew

all those board games, front to back, inside and out. She could practically recite their rulebooks by heart. "Shuttle Quest is missing pieces, but you can make it work," she said, trying not to muffle her voice with her nose. She did that when she was nervous. "The best game, though, is Starhopper Supreme, but—"

Anno turned to look at Jeko, one of her triangular red ears skewing.

Jeko stumbled but managed to get the rest of her sentence out: "—you, uh, need three players to really play it right." Of course, Jeko had played it many times with only herself and two imaginary players. But it would be much more fun with real companions.

Anno pulled the beat-up cardboard box for Starhopper Supreme out from under a pile of other games and shook it lightly. All the pieces inside made a shuffling sound as it shook. She sniffed the dusty box. "These things are so ancient," she woofed. "All my games at home have a holo-projector instead of physical pieces."

"It's still fun, even if it isn't high tech," Jeko mumbled, covering her mouth with her nose.

The way Anno's ear twitched suggested that the canine girl had heard Jeko anyway.

"Just pick something," Am-lei groaned from her desk. Her long body wiggled like she was very uncomfortable.

"Are you okay?" Jeko asked, coiling her nose around her neck nervously. She hoped the worm girl wasn't going to be sick.

"I'm fine," Am-lei said. "I'm going to start my metamorphosis soon, and it means my skin is so itchy!" She rubbed four rows of short arms over the fleshy green skin of her long torso. "My chrysalis body is getting ready on the inside. It makes moving hard. I wish it would get over already!"

"I don't," Anno woofed. She brought Starhopper Supreme

over and dropped it on Am-lei's desk with a satisfying plop. "When you go into your chrysalis, I'll be all alone."

"It'll only last a month or so," Am-lei said, still wriggling in discomfort. "At least, that's what my mom says happened to her. We don't know any other lepidopterans... so, I don't know if it's always like that."

"I don't know anyone else of my species here either," Jeko said. Crossroads Station was mostly populated by Heffen and humans. "Except my parents. Of course."

Anno snorted. "There's nothing *of course* about that. My mom's not Heffen. She's a Woaoo."

Jeko stared blankly at the canine girl.

"Woaoo are marsupials with big fluffy ears," Anno explained. "Look, my family's part of this whole Xeno-Nativity program. So, I'm the only Heffen in it. That's why all the other Heffens in our class think I'm weird."

Jeko decided to be really brave. "Can... Can I play that game with you two?" She pointed at Starhopper Supreme with her long nose, trying not to let it shake.

"Duh," Anno woofed. "You said it takes three, and it sounds like you know the rules. So, I *assumed* you'd explain it to us."

"That way we don't have to read the rules," Am-lei added.

Terrified and buzzing with excitement inside her chest, Jeko got up, moved two rows over, and shoved a desk up to Am-lei's to give them more space for spreading the board game out. She opened the box with her nose and began setting up the pieces.

"Your nose is so neat," Am-lei said. Her multi-faceted dome eyes glowed with appreciation. "After my metamorphosis, I'm going to have a long, curled proboscis instead of my current mouth parts." She wiggled her stubby mandibular mouth parts. "I don't think I'll be able to use it like that though. At least, I don't see my mom use hers that way. But still, it'll be kind of like your nose!"

"I still hate that you're going to be gone for a WHOLE

MONTH," Anno woofed at Am-lei. Then she turned to Jeko and gave the elephant girl an appraising look. "Maybe I'll hang out with you? Now show us how this game works." She picked up one of the pieces and placed it on the wrong side of the board.

Jeko smiled under her nose.

Maybe the glass probability dice weren't real hypercrystals that could let you slide between parallel multi-verses, but it still felt like maybe the universe had granted her wish.

32

VEINS OF BLACK, DUST OF GOLD

AM-LEI HAD BEEN GROWING STIFFER by the day. Her long, green, tubular body was usually lithe and flexible. She could twist her way through the grav-bubble obstacle courses on the Crossroads Space Station playground better than any Heffen children in her class. Their canine bodies couldn't bend in half, twist into a pretzel, or grab onto an extra jungle gym bar with a sixth pair of arms.

Lately though, Am-lei had been barely able to bend at all, and all she wanted to do at recess was drape her stiff, itchy body over her desk and play board games with her two best friends, listlessly moving her plastic tokens over the colorful cardboard with her middlemost pair of arms. She'd beaten Anno and Jeko at Starhopper Supreme three days in a row.

Am-lei didn't think she'd win tomorrow. She didn't think she'd be at school.

For the first time in weeks, her body couldn't stop wiggling. It was the middle of the night; her clone mother was asleep in the other room. But Am-lei had woken up with a pressure in her head and an uncontrollable urge to contort and twist and wriggle about. Her mouth felt gooey and tasted sweet. She moved her mandibular mouthparts and felt the sweet goo overflow and dribble down her face.

Silk. It was her chrysalis silk. It was time. She was terrified and thrilled all at the same time.

The pressure in Am-lei's head built and stabbed until she doubled over. She needed her head down, down below the rest of her. The pounding in her head insisted on it.

She'd always had the uncanny ability to climb up walls. It was probably normal for children of her species, but living on a mostly Heffen space station, her ability to grip a smooth, flat, metal, space station wall with her six hands and climb straight up felt like a superpower. It made the other kids stare at her with awe.

Alone in her bedroom, Am-lei grabbed onto the wall, climbed up to the ceiling, and spat the sticky, sweet goo overflowing her mouth all over her bottom-most feet. She glued herself to the ceiling with spit-silk, and then she let her head drop down. She hung like a seed pod from a tree in the space station's arboretum. And then she began to wriggle, writhing like mad from the itchiness all over and under her fleshy, green skin.

Am-lei contorted and flailed, and the stabbing pain in her head grew. She wanted to take her top-most short arms and scratch her face right off. But suddenly—relief. The green skin of her face split open revealing a smooth crystalline surface underneath. She kept flailing, and the itchy, fleshy skin she'd worn for years split down the middle, bunched up. She writhed her way out of it, pushing it up her body until it was nothing but a crumpled garment gathered around her feet, still glued to the ceiling.

Am-lei hung calmly now. The itching was over. The stabbing pain in her head was gone. So was her face. So were her arms. She was a crystalline shell—a smooth, faceless body lined with pulsing blue veins—beautiful, peaceful, and ready to sleep for a long, long time.

Over the next month, Am-lei's mother came into her room daily. Her mother tenderly touched the crystalline surface of her chrysalis lightly with talon-like hands and gently traced the pulsing blue lines of her developing wings with the tips of quivering antennae. The touch tickled Am-lei, but only slightly. Her mother whispered, "I miss you," and read a chapter to her from *The Adventures of Wipple-Bug and Planet Eater* every night.

Am-lei marked the time by these visits—but even the visits felt fuzzy, like a dream. She didn't see her mother with her eyes directly, but through the gauze of her chrysalis shell and the muzzy haze of her drowsing.

Am-lei dreamed that her friends from school visited her. She dreamed they played board games together, but she couldn't move her pieces without arms. She dreamed that she was back at school, but she couldn't move or talk—only watch while her friends forgot all about her. Some of her dreams were real. At least, Am-lei thought her friends had really visited her and played a board game at her desk, simply to be near her. It was hard to be sure.

Eventually, the chrysalis felt tight around her, and Am-lei felt the urge to wake up. The urge to wriggle and move again.

When she tried to wriggle though, all of her movements came out strangely—her body only bent in a few places now; she could feel it—head, thorax, abdomen instead of one long torso. And her legs... She had half as many, only six now, and they folded awkwardly—all six of them were so long. And tightly trapped. She couldn't move right, so Am-lei pushed and strained.

The crystal shell cracked. Am-lei's new legs finally unfolded. She had talon hands like her mother. She tried to cry out in joy, but her voice tangled inside her newly long, curling proboscis. When she managed to find her voice, the sound of it fluted musically like it never had before. She'd had a child's voice; a caterpillar voice, formed by stubby mouth parts. Now she could sing like a butterfly.

Am-lei let herself down to the floor with long, spindly legs. Now the chrysalis was nothing more than a broken, empty, crystal vase, hanging from the ceiling.

As she stood on the floor, Am-lei's wet wings began to unfurl. They stretched out wide. Yellow, blue, purple, veins of black, and dust of gold. Light shone through the delicate membranes and fell on the floor in pools of refracted color. Am-lei flapped her wings lightly, testing muscles her body didn't use to have. She was an adult now. She could hardly wait to go back to school and show her friends how she'd changed.

33

———

WING DAY

LEE-A-LEI HAD NEVER BEEN to a Wing Day party, much less thrown one herself. The butterfly-like alien crossed her upper-most pair of fuzzy exoskeletal arms and watched her clone-daughter scurry around their quarters, excited, sugar-crazed, and impatient for the guests to arrive.

Am-lei flapped her new wings, throwing herself into the air—she bounced off the ceiling and landed awkwardly on newly-long, spindly legs. A month ago, Am-lei had been a pudgy green caterpillar-babe. At least, Lee-a-lei had thought of her as a babe, even though she was nearly ten years old.

"When do my friends get here?" Am-lei fluted, stumbling over the words with her unfamiliar mouth-parts. Her long proboscis unfurled and re-curled, nearly tangling in her mandibles.

"Soon," Lee-a-lei answered, rearranging the table of refreshments yet again. She hated throwing parties—never knowing which friends would come, which would cancel at the last minute, when exactly they'd arrive, or if they'd all get along. She might be a lepidopteran—a type of sentient butterfly—but she was not a social butterfly.

The door chimed and Am-lei flapped over to answer it, tumbling and tripping along the way. Her wings were beautiful —stained glass windows come to life—but they were ungainly and made her clumsy in the space station's gravity.

Am-lei opened the door, and the human woman on the other side gasped. She put her hand to her mouth, and sparkles of tears sprang to her eyes. "You look just like your mother did before she replaced her wings."

"Of course she does," Lee-a-lei fluted. "She hatched from an unfertilized egg; she might as well be my clone. You know that."

"I know," Amy said. "A grandmother can still be surprised by how beautiful her granddaughter is." Amy held her two fleshy arms out, and Am-lei folded four exoskeletal arms around her in a gentle embrace.

Lee-a-lei knew that Am-lei looked more like her than like her adopted human mother Amy, but it was still her identical daughter who looked strange to Lee-a-lei. Having been raised on a human space station, after being rescued from a wrecked ship by a human woman, Lee-a-lei had spent far more of her life looking at humans than her own species. In fact, until Am-lei had emerged from her chrysalis a few days ago, Lee-a-lei had never seen an adult of her species except in info-casts from a faraway home world she'd never visited. Or in a mirror.

"What can I do to help?" Amy asked.

"I think we're all set up." Lee-a-lei touched the edges of various bowls on the refreshment table nervously with each of her four talon-hands.

Amy stepped close to her daughter and laid a fleshy hand on one of Lee-a-lei's mechanical wings. "I'm sorry you never had a Wing Day party," she said. "I didn't know."

"Neither did I," Lee-a-lei fluted. She didn't blame her mother. Amy had done her best raising an alien child. And honestly, although Lee-a-lei looked nothing like other humans, she felt more like a human than a lepidopteran. She was trying to do better for her daughter, trying to give Am-lei some of the things she'd missed out on, save Am-lei from some of the troubles she'd experienced.

The door chimed again. This time, when Am-lei opened it, a crowd of children poured in—each of them a different species, all of them Am-lei's friends, and each of them thrilled to see how she'd metamorphosed over the last month.

"What was it like being in a cocoon?" an avian boy chirped.

"Was it dark and quiet?" a reptilian girl hissed. "Peaceful?"

"It wasn't a cocoon," Am-lei fluted, flapping her wings so vigorously she rose into the air, tilted, lost balance, and crashed down again. "It was a chrysalis hanging from the ceiling, and when my head split open—"

"WHAT?" the avian squawked.

"My head split open."

It took a while for Am-lei to explain her words to her crowd of friends. Lee-a-lei could sympathize with their horror and confusion. She remembered the metamorphosis happening to herself and had still been terrified as she watched it begin with her own daughter. Am-lei's adorable caterpillar face had split down the middle, crumpled up, and been replaced by a smooth, crystalline shell of a chrysalis underneath. Lee-a-lei couldn't even fathom how her human mother had handled watching that happen to her.

Even so, Am-lei's chrysalis had been the most beautiful thing Lee-a-lei had ever seen.

Under the translucent shell, the lines of Am-lei's caterpillar body had transformed—green curves stretched into blue arcs, growing longer, narrower, more aristocratic and serious over the weeks. Finger-like mouth parts coalesced into a swooping proboscis. In that sleep of metamorphosis, blue veins pulsed, and purple-wet wings developed from tiny buds to crammed-folds, filling the inside of the chrysalis so tightly, so very tightly, it had had to burst open.

Lee-a-lei had felt tentative and unsure at first when Am-lei had emerged in her adult form. She'd looked so different. Lee-a-lei had felt shy with her own daughter, a being who shared her entire genetic code and had spent every day with her for ten years, ever since hatching from an unfertilized yellow egg.

"Wait," the reptilian girl hissed, breaking Lee-a-lei from her reverie. "How did you hang from the ceiling? Was there a hook up there or something?" The reptilian girl craned her neck, looking at every corner of the ceiling, forked tongue flicking.

"Of course not," Am-lei fluted. "I glued my feet to the ceiling with silk-spit from the glands in my mouth."

"Ewwww!!!" all the alien children cried in chorus.

"Now I'm not hungry for any of these snacks!" the avian boy complained. Although he still took a wing-handful of toasted berry-buds.

Lee-a-lei waited until all the guests had arrived and the snacks were nearly demolished before pulling her daughter aside and saying, "I think it's time."

Am-lei flapped her wings and clapped four talon-hands eagerly, practically vibrating with excitement.

She had no reason not to be excited—she'd known all along that the wings she'd grow were vestigial and would need to be removed. Unlike Lee-a-lei, she wouldn't suffer through years of clumsiness, knocking down everything around herself, and slow-growing aches as the too-large wings messed up all the muscles in her back.

This was a good thing.

This was what Amy would have done for Lee-a-lei if she'd known, if she'd been able to locate the lepidopteran home world and get any basic information about her daughter. Instead, she'd muddled through, and it had never occurred to her that lepidopterans removed their wings shortly after growing them.

Even so, Lee-a-lei had lived on Crossroads Station with her

natural, biological wings for years, being constantly praised by humans and other aliens for their beauty. She'd learned to value them for the way they turned her into a work of art that turned every human's head.

And yet, she'd been relieved when she'd learned they could be removed—that it was normal for them to be removed. By then, Lee-a-lei had been so used to her wings that she'd commissioned a much smaller, more useful, mechanical pair to replace them. But Am-lei didn't even want those. She'd read all the info-casts from their home world and had definitely declared: she was going to be a normal, wingless lepidopteran.

Am-lei handed her mother the knife.

With infinite care, Lee-a-lei pressed the metal blade to Am-lei's back where the soft wing membrane met the hard exoskeleton.

Amy turned away.

Lee-a-lei pressed down with the knife and sliced the first wing off in one smooth cut. The membrane parted under the knife as easily as warm butter. The wing fell to the floor. The stained glass window had melted.

Am-lei laughed. "I'm lopsided now!"

All her friends laughed with her.

Lee-a-lei curled her proboscis tightly. It was hard to cut so much beauty away from her daughter, but she knew it shouldn't be. Her daughter was wiser and better informed than she'd been. If she'd been raised in her own culture, this would be a joyous occasion for her too, instead of a bittersweet one.

"Cut the other one, cut the other one!" Am-lei led the other children in a chant.

Lee-a-lei's hand-talon shook, holding the knife. She didn't know if she could do that again.

A fleshy human hand steadied Lee-a-lei's talon, and the lepidopteran looked up to see the face of her mother. "Let me,"

Amy said. "I should have done this for you. Let me be a part of doing it for your daughter."

"Thank you," Lee-a-lei fluted, handing over the knife. She stepped back to watch.

Amy cut off Am-lei's second wing, and it fell discarded to the floor. All the children cheered, and Am-lei pirouetted, spindly exoskeletal arms waving like she was leading a choir.

34

WHAT THE EYES COVET AND THE STOMACH CRAVES

LIKE A DELICATE CRYSTAL VASE, the hard shell of Am-lei's chrysalis cracked, spilling out the furled up, new-grown, riotously colorful wings inside. Still wet, the wings hung from her changed body, pulsing with life, heavy and dragging her down, out of the chrysalis that had held her, dormant, for the last month.

The month had passed like a dream. Am-lei remembered her body itching all over, and her mouth overflowing with gooey silk-spittle. She remembered climbing up the walls of her room and gluing her feet to the ceiling as her squishy, green caterpillar skin split down the middle, shedding like a winter coat on a hot day, revealing the hardened chrysalis that had developed underneath, her new outer shell, as the rest of her melted and mutated inside.

Those memories were sharp and clear, and even to her, a little horrifying. It had felt natural, but she'd grown up with enough mammalian, avian, and reptilian friends to know that your face splitting open and peeling off is supposed to be the stuff of horror films.

But the memories afterward... Her mother visiting every

night, and reading stories to her. Her best friends—an elephantine alien and canine alien—coming and playing board games beside her dormant shell. Those images were fuzzy in her mind, seen through the obscuring veil of her chrysalis.

As Am-lei rested on the bed beneath where her broken, twisted shell of a chrysalis still hung, she sorted through the memories and the dreams, trying to figure out what had been real, and what she'd imagined. Until hunger overcame her.

"I haven't eaten in a month," Am-lei tried to say, but her mouth was so different that the words came out as a jumble of incoherent, fluting sounds. Pretty but ineffectual. She lifted a talon to her face. Her arms were long now—they'd been stubby before—and they ended in hard, exoskeleton-covered talons, not pudgy caterpillar hands. But her face was even more different.

The wriggling mouthparts she remembered were still there, but smaller, more vestigial; and her mandibles had shrunk to mere relics of what they used to be. All of it made way for her new mouth—the long, curling, flute-like proboscis. Like her mother's. She had an adult body now, with an adult face, and an adult mouth.

Her mother, Lee-a-lei, appeared at the door, holding a goblet of golden liquid. The ambrosia adult lepidopterans drank.

Am-lei accepted the goblet greedily. She unfurled her proboscis clumsily, taking three tries to land the end of it in the goblet where she could suck up the sticky, sweet goodness through her new mouth like a straw.

The golden fluid settled in her stomach, soothing the roar of hunger, but leaving her uneasy. Everything felt strange and off. She'd never thought about how her stomach or limbs or most of her body really felt before... She'd simply lived in it, and all those parts had done what she told them to do. But now, she went to move her arm, and since it was longer, it moved farther and faster than she meant. She tried to speak, and the parts of her face fell all over each other, trying to fulfill the commands sent by her brain, but not quite getting them right.

Lee-a-lei sat down beside her clone-daughter, taking back the empty goblet. "It takes a while to settle into your new body."

"It must have been scary for you," Am-lei said. Her mother had been rescued as an infant caterpillar from a crashed space-ship and raised by the human woman who found her. Neither of them had known she would go through a chrysalis phase. Nor that lepidopterans generally cut off their wings during a coming-of-age celebration after emerging.

Lepidopterans considered their wings vestigial. Without any adult lepidopterans around, though, Lee-a-lei had lived with the inconvenient yet beautiful appendages weighing her down for many years.

Lee-a-lei traced the dark veins on Am-lei's quivering, still-drying wings with the tip of a talon. "So beautiful," she said.

"Do you still miss yours, Mother?"

"Sort of." Lee-a-lei drew her talon back, as if the bright pools of color in Am-lei's wings could burn her. "Most humans look at me differently now."

"You're just a big bug, not a beautiful butterfly."

"Right."

Am-lei could read the sadness in her mother's slouched arms, all four of them, and the tight, pinched curl of her proboscis. "To hell with humans, though, right?" Am-lei said, trying to cheer her up. "Well, I mean, except for Grandma."

"She'll be here shortly," Lee-a-lei said. "To help us get ready for the party."

All of Am-lei's school friends came to her Wing Day party. Children of all species—a perfect cross-section of Crossroads Station's inhabitants—crashed through the lepidopterans' apartment, shouting, tussling, carousing, and generally having fun.

Lee-a-lei and her adoptive mother, Amy, put out trays and bowls of snacks, and kept refilling them as the guests devoured the tasty morsels. Toasted berry-buds, kernels of soft cheese, fried sweet breads, and smoked fingerling fishes. Amy had been cooking all night, ever since she'd heard that Am-lei's chrysalis had begun to crack.

The star of the party bounced and floated through the room, flapping her vestigial wings or trying to glide with them. Her best friend, Jeko the elephantine alien, held a flashlight in her trunk and shone its beam through Am-lei's left wing, casting pools of colored light all over the assembled children who oohed and ahhed at how pretty they were. Like stained glass windows, come to life.

When the time came for her wings to be cut off, Am-lei didn't flinch or hesitate. Though, both her lepidopteran mother and human grandmother did. The knife sliced through the soft flesh of the wing, along the hard edge of her exo-skeletal cara-pace, as smoothly as through warm butter. Lee-a-lei cut off the first wing, leaving her daughter lopsided and laughing, a wondrous, fluting sound with her new mouth; Amy took the knife and cut off the other.

After the last guest left, Am-lei curled up on the couch, all four, long arms wrapped around her swollen abdomen and groaned.

Amy worked on clearing away the remnants of the food she'd brought, but Lee-a-lei came over to kneel beside her daughter, who looked more like a mirror of her today than ever before. "What's wrong, love?" she asked. "Do you miss your wings? You didn't get to keep them for very long. Not like I did."

Am-lei laughed like a squashed bagpipe, less musical and more a snort of derision. "Are you kidding? Those things were crazy awkward. I don't know how you put up with them all those years."

"Are you sad the party's over?" Lee-a-lei asked, gently running a talon along one of Am-lei's curved antennae. "Or maybe you're hungry and need more nectar?"

Am-lei groaned. "No, I've eaten enough."

Amy stood by the door, arms filled with containers of leftovers, looking sympathetically at her alien daughter and granddaughter. Just an old human woman who loved her progeny as much as any grandmother could, regardless of their wildly different bodies. "I'm going to take the leftovers home, and see you both tomorrow. Okay?"

"Wait," Am-lei said, "you're not taking all of them are you?" Her grandmother and the armful of packaged up tasty treats reflected in every facet of her silvery, disco ball-like eyes.

"Well, yes," Amy said. "I didn't figure you'd have much use for them."

"But..." Am-lei objected, confused.

"You weren't eating the snacks for the guests, were you?" Lee-a-lei asked, her own proboscis curling tightly and antennae waving worriedly.

"Well... yeah?" Am-lei groaned again, as a sharp pain in her abdomen doubled her over even more tightly.

Human grandmother and lepidopteran mother exchanged a glance.

"Oh dear," Amy said, sighing. "You've got a long night ahead of you. Good luck." And she left the two lepidopterans alone. The only two butterflies—albeit without wings—on a space station full of mammals, avians, and reptiles.

"Honey, have you ever seen me eat solid food?" Lee-a-lei asked.

"Well, no... but... I thought you just didn't like it?"

Lee-a-lei sat on the couch beside her curled up daughter and stroked the gleaming, new carapace with gentle talons. "I guess I should have talked about this more," she said. "I hadn't realized..." With a deep sigh, she straightened out her antennae, steeling her resolve. She hadn't talked enough about her past before, so she would have to talk about it now. "I'm sorry, I guess it was just too painful for me. Of course, I ate solid food as a caterpillar, and then... because I didn't know better, I kept eating it after my chrysalis."

Am-lei didn't like where this was going. Part of her knew. Part of her had known before she popped the toasted berry-buds in the vestigial mouth under her proboscis. Part of her had felt her body rebel against their solidity. Their delicious, complicated texture. But she didn't want to believe it, so she'd choked down kernels of cheese and pieces of sweet bread too. They'd tasted as delicious as ever. Maybe even more delicious, because they'd also tasted... dangerous. Like she wasn't supposed to be eating them, and that extra edge had made them special.

"Adult lepidopteran stomachs aren't suited to solid foods."

Am-lei hated hearing her mother say that sentence out loud, as if refusing to say it would make it untrue. "Then what I am I supposed to do?" she wailed, remembering every food she'd ever loved; every meal that she'd shared with her friends; every moment of joy she'd felt while munching on a simple snack, letting her wriggling mouth parts play with the toasty leaves of a berry bud, pulling it apart and savoring each leaf as she ate it.

She was never going to do that again. The meals she'd eaten before hardening into her chrysalis should have been her last. And based on how her swollen abdomen felt—like it would explode any moment and leave her to die—the ones she'd eaten today really would be her last.

The part of her life when she got to eat toasted berry buds, and soft, oozy cheeses, and sugar encrusted rolls were all over.

Birthday cakes at her friends' parties.

Slurping up long spaghetti noodles.

Her best friend Jeko throwing popcorn at her with her trunk, and Am-lei catching it with her mouth parts.

It was all over.

She hadn't expected it to ever end.

"You'll drink nectar," Lee-a-lei said, simply. And it felt profoundly unfair.

Am-lei groaned and rocked her abdomen. The swaying motion seemed to help. The groaning helped too—it was half pain, and half disconsolate loss.

After a while, her groaning and the pain causing it subsided a little, and Am-lei said, "How did you... figure it out?"

"It took years," Lee-a-lei admitted.

"Years?" Am-lei asked in alarm. She couldn't imagine suffering this kind of pain for years. She desperately didn't want to give up solid foods, but she also couldn't imagine letting another piece of solid food past her mandibles again. Not ever. This pain was too much.

"I was very sick for the first few years after my chrysalis," Lee-a-lei said. "It took months and months of trial and error, experimenting with different foods and combinations, sometimes spending days in the medical center under observation, before I figured out what I could safely eat. In the end, it was your grandmother who figured it out, actually. Not me. I don't think I wanted to see the truth."

"I can understand that." Am-lei curled her proboscis tightly. She hated this—both the pain and the change. But what her mother had been through sounded so much worse.

"Did you see the gift your grandmother brought for you?" Lee-a-lei asked, stroking Am-lei's antennae again.

Am-lei lifted her head from the arm of the couch, sparkling disco-ball eyes trying to see where there might be a present lying around, waiting for her. "Wing Day isn't really a gift-giving holiday," she said.

"I know," Lee-a-lei agreed, getting up from the couch. She went over to a table by the door and lifted a small rectangular box, about the size of terran grapefruit, wrapped in colorful paper. She brought it over and offered it to her daughter.

Am-lei sat up, intrigued enough by the gift to forget the ache in her abdomen for a moment. She tore off the paper and found a mechanical object inside.

"It's a travel-size blender," Lee-a-lei explained. "I used to carry one with me, when I was still adapting to... an adult lepidopteran diet. I'll warn you—most foods that your friends eat won't be nearly as good once they're blended. But..."

"It lets me participate."

"Yeah, also, it lets you..." Lee-a-lei shrugged her four arms in frustration. "I don't know. It made it easier to let go? If you can still eat the food, but only in a way where it doesn't taste good... it's easier to lie to yourself and pretend you just don't like it anymore."

A tentative, fluting laugh came from Am-lei. "That's kind of sad, Mom."

"I know. It still helped. And you know, you can still drink all the beverages that your friends enjoy—tea, coffee, smoothies, soda pop."

"Huh," Am-lei mused, "I wonder how carbonation feels now." She ran a talon along the curve of her proboscis.

"Want to find out?" Lee-a-lei's antennae curled toward each other, sketching out a vaguely heart-shape in the air. She knew that carbonation was delightfully ticklish inside an adult lepidopteran proboscis, even more so than in a caterpillar-stage mouth. It could also be soothing on a swollen abdomen, distended by solid foods it wasn't designed to process anymore. "I'll get you something, okay?"

Am-lei put the blender down on the floor next to the couch and laid herself back down again. "Yeah, Mom, thanks."

When Lee-a-lei brought her daughter a tall glass of sugary, fizzy soda pop—her favorite flavor, Centauri Citrus—the newly adult-bodied lepidopteran took the drink in her talons, unfurled her proboscis into the glass, and felt the tickly bubbles all over both the inside and outside of her new straw-like mouth. The sweetness and tart bite of citrus was more intense flowing through the curve of her proboscis than it had ever been in her caterpillar mouth, and while she sipped it down, she thought about all the foods she used to enjoy, almost flinching at the thought of them now.

She would have to learn the difference between the foods her eyes coveted and the ones her stomach craved. Hopefully, eventually, she could get them to align. She would shed her desire for the foods of her caterpillar stage the same way she had shed her wings today. Wings that were beautiful... but ultimately useless to her.

At least, while she was settling into this new way of life, she'd be in her cool new body with a shiny exo-skeletal carapace, long limbs, and a proboscis that made her voice sound like a beautiful, musical instrument.

35

JETPACK AND CYBORG WINGS

LEE-A-LEI and her clone-daughter Am-lei perched in the Crossroads Station recreational airlock with their long spindly legs folded. The two lepidopterans exchanged a glance with glittering, multi-faceted eyes. Lee-a-lei was nervous and kept flapping her mechanical wings, but her daughter looked excited.

Am-lei didn't have wings. She'd followed the traditions of their homeworld and had her yellow-blue-and-purple wings cut off after she metamorphosed. So, she wore a simple zero-gee jetpack like a human or one of the canine Heffens would. The jetpack strapped around her thorax, firmly secured. Lee-a-lei had checked her daughter's straps several times.

Neither of them wore spacesuits—their exoskeletons protected most of their bodies, and a thin coating of amphiphilic goo around their joints sealed the gaps up well enough for an hour long joy-jaunt around the station's exterior. An oxygen mask strapped over each lepidopteran's curling proboscis was the only other thing they'd needed to transform from planet-dwellers to vacuum-dwellers.

"Isn't this thrilling?" Am-lei fluted inside her oxygen mask.

Lee-a-lei heard her daughter's words through a radio strapped over her tympanal organ on the side of her thorax. The sound was muddied though by the vibration of the airlock floor under her talons. The doors would open soon.

A deep rumble, and then whoosh.

The thin air behind Lee-a-lei shoved her out the opening airlock doors. It was a waste of air, but the algae-filters on the station were extremely effective, and Crossroads got regular shipments of fresh air from the closest planet. So, a little air lost to make the ride more fun? No big deal. Life on a space station should be fun. Hell, life of any sort should be fun.

Lee-a-lei flapped her mechanical wings; there was no air outside the space station for them to push against, but the movement of her muscles triggered the jetpack function of her wings. She zoomed along the curve of the station, following her fearless daughter.

Lee-a-lei had been raised by a well-meaning but clueless human. By the time they discovered it was normal for lepidopterans to cut off their beautiful but vestigial wings, Lee-a-lei no longer felt like herself without them. So, she'd gotten specially-fitted mechanical wings—much smaller and more useful, but they let her still feel like herself. A butterfly. That's how the humans she'd been raised around had always seen her, and it was how she'd come to see herself.

Now she was a butterfly—a cyborg butterfly—flying through the velvety blackness of space! Am-lei was right: it was thrilling.

Lee-a-lei flapped faster, and the jets in her cyborg wings pushed her forward in tiny bursts that matched the flaps. She flew away from the shiny metal walls and transparent aluminum windows of Crossroads Station until she could see its concentric rings, turning and twisting like a gyroscope, as a whole. It looked like a child's toy, discarded on a black sand beach. The stars and planets of the local solar system gleamed with the natural beauty of seashells, and space stretched away like an ocean in every direction.

Lee-a-lei lived her life inside that toy.

Swooping back toward her daughter, Lee-a-lei fluted, "It makes you feel small, doesn't it?"

"Not me," Am-lei answered. The younger lepidopteran had figured out how to use alternating bursts from one side and then the other of her jetpack to fly in zig-zagging curlicues. Her six long legs waved grandiosely, as if she were trying to greet every star she saw. Their celestial light glittered on the many facets of her eyes. "I'm going to see all of it someday."

I hope you do, Lee-a-lei thought. What she said was, "Take me with you."

"Of course!" Am-lei spun around with her jetpack and zoomed up to her mother. The young lepidopteran grasped the older lepidopteran's uppermost left talon with one of her own. The two butterflies—one with a jetpack instead of wings and the other with cyborg wings—flew together around the space station that was their home.

36

A JETPACK OF A DIFFERENT COLOR

WENDY SHIFTED the jetpack on her shoulders and knocked on the door to Flooffle's quarters. After three knocks and no response, Wendy called out, "Come on! I want to hit the ammonia waves on New Jupiter before the lava moon freezes over!"

Flooffle still didn't answer, so Wendy keyed in the security code, and the door slid aside. She expected to find her fuzzy six-legged friend inside, struggling to get a jetpack settled onto the back of his carapace.

Instead Flooffle crouched stock still on the center of the floor, his six legs folded together, and his head leaned forward. His fuzzy blue fur had turned eerily white—almost crystalline.

"Are you okay?" Wendy asked, reaching toward her friend. The way his body was curled forward, Flooffle looked like he was in pain. Wendy touched his mid-left leg lightly, and it crumbled to dust.

Wendy cried out and fell backwards, losing her balance as the weight of her jetpack pulled her down. Her foot flew forward—she didn't feel an impact, but Flooffle's furry body dissolved like dust particles in sunlight.

Her friend was gone.

"Ready to go?" It was Flooffle's voice, except higher and purer.

Wendy looked up to see a smooth-carapaced, six-legged alien twice Flooffle's height and azure blue. Not the same blue. Flooffle's fur had been a comfortable, faded shade. This was a deep, gleaming turquoise.

"Is that you, Flooffle?" Wendy asked, finally pulling herself together and getting up off the floor. "What the hell happened?"

"I decided to molt into my adult form. I'm a queen not a drone. It's Fleia now." Fleia turned to the side, displaying a pair of shimmering wings. "Growing wings seemed easier than finding a jetpack to fit me. Now, come on, we've got some atmo-surfing to do."

37

THE SEAMSTRESS ROBOT AND THE INSECT BRIDE

THE SEAMSTRESS ROBOT'S shop was a little hole in the wall in the Merchant's Quarter of Crossroads Station. The seamstress robot herself looked a lot like a giant mechanical spider—all spindly silver legs, overly jointed and coming to extremely delicate points, capable of grabbing, manipulating, and piercing fabric. Also, generating fabric. The seamstress robot, like an actual spider, could generate silk. And synthetic cotton. And synth wool. And velvet, taffeta, patterned prints, fake leather... just about any material you could imagine could be generated, strand by strand, from the tip of her 3D printer leg.

The seamstress robot was one of Maradia's finest inventions —just shy of sentient, but extremely competent. Over the centuries, sewing had turned out to be one of the absolute hardest crafts to automate, as it involves extremely delicate, precise physical movements that vary so much from one to the next and involve such complexity that an adept mind must carefully monitor them, constantly adjusting. But finally, well after humans had explored and colonized the stars, Maradia had managed to automate sewing.

After creating the seamstress robot, Maradia had set SR01 —as the robot liked to be called—up with a little shop, which of course stayed registered in Maradia's name, since the robot (being less than sentient) couldn't own anything herself. SR01's shop more than paid for itself, in spite of the fact that most humans and Heffens living on the station considered the robot herself very creepy and unnerving, far too insectile with her many—far too many, more than a spider, and constantly moving so very hard to count—overly jointed legs.

Am-lei, however, being an insectoid alien herself, found SR01's physical presence rather comforting, which was good, because she was feeling very nervous about picking out a wedding dress for herself. She was used to the humans and canine Heffens who lived aboard Crossroads Station treating her like some kind of nightmare vision, until they got to know her. That hadn't been true back when she'd been a pudgy green caterpillar—back then, everyone had found her adorable. Then she'd spent a month inside a chrysalis and emerged looking almost exactly like her mother—long spindly legs; hard shiny exoskeleton; and glittering many-faceted eyes.

Am-lei's mother had, at least, enjoyed the benefit of having beautiful, colorful, butterfly wings that distracted humans from the Kafkaesque qualities of her actual body. But then Am-lei's mother had been an orphan foundling, adopted by a well-meaning but ignorant human who didn't know her wings were vestigial and her species, Lepidopterans, traditionally cut them off.

Am-lei had known about her species' traditions, and rather than suffer years of heavy wings messing up the muscles in her back and bumping against everything, she'd emerged from her chrysalis to a celebratory Wing Day party where her mother had ceremonially sliced off one of her wings with a knife, and then her human grandmother had sliced off the other one. Am-lei didn't regret cutting her wings off. But she was sometimes jealous of the years her mother had spent looking like an ethereal angel to the humans who surrounded her... instead of plunging straight into looking like a Cthonian devil.

What must it have been like to walk through life admired by all around her for her incredible beauty? Am-lei had never known.

But Jeko thought she was beautiful. And most days, that was more than enough for Am-lei. To have captured the heart of a gentle, shy, sweet elephantine woman? Any lady should be so lucky.

Jeko held up a colorful piece of silk with her trunk—a sample of fabric—and said, "What about this? It would look nice."

Am-lei shrugged her four long, spindly arms. Nothing here was inspiring her, no matter how many swaths of sample fabric SRo1 wove for her. No matter how many mock-up dresses SRo1 draped over her angular body.

Jeko had already found a wedding dress that suited her—white with gold edging, gathered skirt that came to just above her hoof-like toes, and long, tight elegant sleeves. She looked gorgeous in it—her plump curves perfectly flattered by the gauzy fabric. She far outshone any of the human brides Am-lei had seen, both in real life and the old movies her human grandmother liked to watch. Human faces looked boring without long trunks hanging expressively from them, and their smooth, tight skin looked plastic and fake compared to Jeko's wrinkly gray folds.

Lepidopterans didn't usually pair-bond, according to what Am-lei had read about her people, and so there was no cultural ceremony from her people for braiding two lives together with the ribbons of romantic love; Jeko's elephantine species did have their own versions of wedding ceremonies, but Jeko's parents had traveled so much when she'd been little that she'd never felt attached to her own species' traditions.

Am-lei and Jeko had settled on a fairly typical human-style ceremony with fancy gowns and promises spoken aloud, because they'd both spent so much time living among humans. Besides, Am-lei's Grandma Amy was loving it, and it was always fun to make Grandma Amy happy.

Grandma Amy had even tried to convince Am-lei to let her help pick out the wedding dress, but the brides had wanted to pick the dresses out together... just the two of them.

"I don't know, Jeko," Am-lei said. "No matter what kind of fabric we try, or how we wrap it around me... I still just feel like some kind of nightmare vision when we put me in a fancy ball gown of any sort. It doesn't usually get to me..."

Jeko put down the scrap of fabric she'd been holding in her trunk and stared quietly at Am-lei, focusing on her completely.

Am-lei felt the muscles in the joints between her different pieces of exoskeleton relax a little. She always felt better when Jeko looked at her—really looked at her—like she could see all the way down to Am-lei's heart, pumping hemolymph through her body—yellow-green where a human's blood would be red.

"I know what I look like to most of the mammal species on Crossroads Station, and I don't care most of the time. I know who I am... But this just feels like some kind of horror-movie dress-up game. Like, let's put the big bug in human clothes! Maybe we could even cut off some human skin to drape over her hideous hard carapace! Then she'd be a real bride!"

Jeko didn't say anything. She didn't have to. Am-lei knew when she was being ridiculous and going overboard.

"What about a suit?" Jeko asked, pointing with her trunk to one of the displays that SRo1 had pulled up on a wall-screen while suggesting things she could sew for them.

SRo1 saw the gesture and matched it with one of her long mechanical arms. "Yes, I can make suits." Her spindly arm reached to the controls for the wall-screen, and suddenly the image of a human bride and groom standing next to each other was replaced with an image of five different people—three humans, a Heffen, and a koala-like alien—all wearing different styles of suits with sleek, sharp angles. Classy vests, straight-cut legs, and brightly colored neckties providing the one color contrast to otherwise simple gray-tone pieces.

Am-lei turned away. Though, with her disco-ball-like eyes, she could still see the image behind her. Turning away was a physical gesture she'd learned from spending time around mammaloids and other aliens who could only see forward. She knew it worked differently for them... but it still felt like an effective way to communicate what she was feeling sometimes.

"Okay," Jeko said. "I guess that's still playing dress-up-the-bug, huh?"

Am-lei shrugged again. She knew that shrugging looked extra impressive on her, with her extra arms. She wasn't trying to be melodramatic. She just didn't like any of the options being presented to her, and it was starting to make her wonder if she belonged participating in a human-style wedding cere-mony at all. Just because Grandma Amy was excited about it, and Jeko was having the time of her life planning everything didn't mean... well... it didn't mean they had to have a human-style wedding. But... It was wonderful watching Jeko get so excited about every detail of the planning. It had been drawing them even closer together—picking a menu for the reception afterward, selecting decorations, choosing a location. It was all a lot of fun.

But... this part made Am-lei feel left out. The idea of dressing up like a mammal didn't make Am-lei feel fancy and special the way that Jeko's gown clearly made her feel. It made her feel fake and wrong.

But the idea of wearing anything like her usual clothes—mostly just scarves tied and draped around her carapace—just didn't feel special enough. She didn't know what to do. She didn't want to ruin all of this for Jeko… but she also didn't want to play along and pretend to be happy when she wasn't really feeling that way.

If anyone had known how to dress a body like Am-lei's for a formal occasion, she would have thought it would be SR01 with her similarly spindly, angular, insectile form. And yet, watching SR01 clamber around her small shop, gathering up the swaths of fabric strewn everywhere and carefully folding them back into neatly organized piles, Am-lei realized the robot probably never had any occasions to dress up for.

SR01 lived here, in her shop. She lived to serve the customers who came looking for personally tailored clothing. She didn't actually live. She was just a robot.

How simple and clear—to have a purpose and do nothing other than serve that purpose.

Maybe Am-lei's people were right—romantic pair-bonding was a distraction, and she should simply focus on her work as a physicist. Being here in this dress shop wasn't making her happy. Jeko made her happy, but did they really need a whole special ceremony to codify that? They could be happy together without trying to painfully force their feelings for each other into some box that was designed for an entirely different species, dating way back to when that species had lived in isolation on the single planetary cradle they'd crawled into the rest of the universe from.

"Maybe we just shouldn't do this…" Am-lei fluted the words quietly, keeping her proboscis coiled as she spoke them. She didn't want to say them. She didn't want them to be heard. But the words had seemed to leak out of her anyway, reflecting feelings too strong to be denied.

Jeko reached out her trunk, placed it on Am-lei's narrow shoulders, and guided her conflicted, troubled, insectile fiancé to turn back toward her. "We're doing this because it's fun. What can we do to make this fun for you?"

"None of this feels like me," Am-lei fluted. "I don't feel like me while I'm doing this. But... I don't know what would feel like me."

"Well, let's think about you," Jeko said.

In the background, SR01 continued to busy herself with tidying the shop, giving the brides a little privacy. Though, given the robot's sub-sentience, neither bride was too worried about her listening in. SR01 knew how to be companionable and polite, but when someone wasn't specifically talking to her, that part of herself seemed to shut down. She wasn't an inherently social being; she simply had subroutines for being reactively social when necessary as part of her guiding purpose, namely designing and creating practical, wearable works of art out of soft fabrics.

"You're a brilliant physicist," Jeko said, still staring at Am-lei with her small, bright eyes in a way that said, "I see all of you, every piece of you, and I love it all."

"Okay, sure, but that doesn't really help us here?" Am-lei fluted.

"You say you hate poetry, but you actually love it... you're just really particular about which pieces you like. You're fiercely competitive when you play games, but you feel like you shouldn't be, so you try to hide it as much as possible. And you're extremely conflicted about your Lepidopteran heritage, partly because you like how special it makes you that you're one of only two Lepidopterans on Crossroads Station but mostly because you're afraid that, having been raised among so many mammaloids, you somehow don't deserve access to a cultural heritage that you've mostly only read about."

If Am-lei had the kind of eyes that would let her look away from Jeko, she would have then. Jeko's words pierced too close to her heart.

"But you are a Lepidopteran, and you do deserve that cultural heritage, even if that means putting your own spin on it. So, let's figure out how you can make this mish-mashed human-style wedding twisted around for an elephant and a butterfly into something that feels like *yours*."

Am-lei always found it a little funny when Jeko referred to the two of them as an "elephant and butterfly." Yes, Jeko and her parents looked *a lot* like the animals that humans called elephants. But Am-lei had only really looked like a butterfly for one day in her life—the day she'd emerged from her chrysalis and attended her Wing Day party. By the end of the party, she hadn't really looked like a butterfly anymore, because that had been all about the wings. Sure, she looked like some kind of giant insect, but from what she understood about humans and the animals they liked to compare everything to, butterflies were really all about the big, colorful, beautiful wings.

And she didn't have those.

But... maybe she could.

"I have an idea," Am-lei fluted. She leaned away from Jeko, focusing instead on the robot who was currently busying herself with a tray of spools and bobbins full of thread in a whole rainbow of colors. "Can you pull up some images of the animal that humans call 'butterfly'?"

"Of course," SRo1 answered pleasantly. Three of her spindly legs moved quickly to work various control panels around the room, and suddenly every wall-screen around them filled with bright, colorful pictures of all sorts of butterflies. Monarchs in orange and black; swallowtails in yellow with gemstone touches of purple and blue; checkerboard-colored wings; simple white wings with only a small touch of black and red like an eye in the corner; and so many, many more.

Am-lei pointed to the white-winged butterfly. It was smaller and simpler than the other butterflies around it, but its white wings made her think of all the white wedding gowns she and

Jeko had been looking at. "What if instead of a gown... I wore cloth wings?"

"I think that's a lovely idea," Jeko said.

"Could you make something like those wings?" Am-lei asked the robot. "For me to wear?"

SRoi didn't answer right away, not with words, at least. Instead, she put down the tray of thread, clambered back toward Am-lei, and then took hold of the insect bride's foremost arms with her own metal arms. SRoi gently spread Am-lei's arms wide, lowered them, positioned them at a few different angles, and then let go. SRoi stepped back and looked at Am-lei for a moment, seemingly pondering. Given her high-speed electronic brain, she was probably running through hundreds or even thousands of design schematics for possible wing patterns in the few seconds it took her to finally provide an answer: "Yes, I recommend we attach the wings to your arms in a few locations, then they will move with you. A little like a cape, but more involved. Shall I spin you a mock-up?"

"Sure," Am-lei answered, finally feeling a glimmer of hope about these proceedings. She was still worried she wouldn't like whatever SRoi came up with... but, actually, that wasn't quite right. She wasn't just worried. She was actually a little scared, because this time, the idea behind the garment actually spoke to her.

Am-lei liked the idea of wearing wings to her wedding. She'd worn wings on the day of her last big rite of passage—a Wing Day party was truly, in Lepidopteran culture, the celebration of a child entering adulthood. She'd no longer been a pudgy baby caterpillar; she'd been her adult self for the first time. And her wings—her natural, biological wings—had been the adornment she'd worn to that party.

Am-lei liked the idea of wearing wings—different, fabricated ones—to the big party that would celebrate her and Jeko committing their hearts and futures to each other.

It wasn't a Lepidopteran tradition. But it could be her tradition. Wings for rites of passage.

While Am-lei pondered, SR01 worked busily around her, mechanical legs moving almost too fast to see as she wove simple mock-up wings right onto Am-lei's arms like a giant spider spinning a web onto her.

The wings came out simple—opaque white ovals that hung from her arms and fluttered with her every movement. They weren't like her own wings had been—although they'd been vestigial, those wings had been a part of her. She'd been able to move them and feel them. These wings weren't a part of her. But they adorned her, making her feel a little more like the self she remembered being as an overly excitable, dramatic teenager, high on the idea that finally she was the adult she'd always been meant to become.

This was the bride Am-lei was meant to be. "Yes," she fluted. "I like this, but... could we make the wings less round? And maybe make the fabric a little more translucent... still white, but sort of... gossamer?"

SR01 didn't even bother to answer; she simply launched right into removing the first mock-up wings from Am-lei's arms and sewing the next ones. Just like Am-lei had described them.

After several iterations, changing small details, altering the shape of the pattern and the texture of the fabric, Am-lei found herself wearing a pair of lacy, translucent white wings that made her feel just as fancy and special as Jeko's dress seemed to make her feel.

"You look beautiful," Jeko said.

"Less like a butterfly," Am-lei fluted. "More like... what are those other insects humans talk about?"

"Dragonflies," SR01 offered, and with a small adjustment, pictures of dragonflies appeared on one of the wall-screens. Their wings shimmered in the sunlight.

Am-lei and Jeko wouldn't be getting married under true

sunlight, because they'd chosen to have their wedding aboard Crossroads Station. But the location they'd chosen aboard the station was in the arboretum, and the lamplight in there looked a lot like natural sunlight.

As she exchanged her vows with her beloved elephant, Amlei's dragonfly-like wings would shimmer too.

38

THE ELEPHANT BRIDE'S BOUQUET

JEKO LIFTED her trunk and trumpeted along with the latest Star-Shaker song which she'd turned up to completely fill her small room aboard Crossroads Station. Her trunk swayed along with the beat, and the reptilian pop-star's lilting, raspy voice was loud enough that Jeko didn't have to feel embarrassed about her own brassy tones. The elephantine alien never sang in front of other people, but she loved to sing when she was alone. Especially when she was happy.

And she was filled with joy today.

Today, Jeko was marrying her insect bride—a brilliant, glittering butterfly-like alien who was too fabulous to need wings. Jeko had loved Am-lei from the moment she saw the freshly metamorphosed insect girl standing with one wing—the other already cut from her back at her Wing Day party—and announced, "I'm lopsided!"

When you've loved someone that long—since childhood, the love evolving as you both grow—and they've loved you almost as long, it's almost strange to marry them. Redundant and unnecessary. Just some weird performance, put on for other people, friends and family, but it's also a big, fun, celebratory party. And while Jeko was usually too shy to like parties, she liked the idea of a party all about how much she loved Am-lei, and Am-lei loved her back. Because that was the biggest miracle in her otherwise kind of lonely and solitary life.

Jeko's parents had dragged her from one planet to another, between space stations and asteroid colonies, throughout her whole childhood. Crossroads Station had been just one more lonely stop along the way, until she'd met Am-lei. Then young Jeko had put her heavy foot down: she was done moving. By the time her parents had tried to drag her away from Crossroads Station, Jeko was old enough that she simply stayed behind, finished high school on her own, and made herself a home of her own.

Sure, Am-lei had gone away to college at Wespirtech for awhile, and Jeko had stayed behind, lonely again. But after a few years, Am-lei came back, and the two of them had been together ever since. Elephant and butterfly. Against all odds.

Jeko stopped singing long enough to grab her white wedding dress and pull it over her head. She reached around with her trunk to zip it up and fasten all the decorative gold clasps, wondering as she always did how mammaloids without trunks got by with their mere two arms. At least Am-lei had four arms with her insectile body, though those arms were too stiff and spindly to reach around her own back the way Jeko's trunk could.

Most of the people Jeko knew only had two arms, and it just seemed so limiting.

As soon as Jeko was finished dressing, a knock came on her door. Jeko turned the music down and called out, "Come in!"

Jeko's beautiful butterfly bride floated into the room with gossamer wings, white and gauzy. They weren't real wings. Only part of her dress, an affectation designed to make her feel more like herself on this celebratory day. The last really big celebration in her life had been her Wing Day party, when she'd emerged from her chrysalis all wobbly on those six spindly new limbs and weighed down by big colorful wings.

During Am-lei's Wing Day party, her mother had cut off one of her natural wings, and her grandmother cut off the second one.

Tonight, Jeko would get to remove Am-lei's wedding wings. The elephantine alien felt the insides of her large, flappy ears blush at the thought. Even though it was just the two of them alone—Jeko and her Am-lei—she could still blush at the idea of being allowed to love such a beautiful, delicate creature.

"Your dress is perfect," Jeko said, curling her trunk nervously around her own neck.

"I feel silly," Am-lei fluted, curling her proboscis up tightly in a mirror of Jeko's curled up trunk. "Fake wings? It's silly."

Both brides were nervous. Neither had any reason to be. They loved each other, and only their closest friends and family were coming to the wedding. Even so, it's strange to be in the center of a spotlight. It's a strange feeling, inviting people to a party in celebration of yourself. Especially for a shy elephant like Jeko.

"It's not silly to wear wings," Jeko trumpeted, trying to soothe her beloved. "Your mother still wears those prosthetic mechanical wings."

Am-lei's mother Lee-a-lei—having been raised by a human —hadn't learned about their species' tradition of cutting their wings off until much later in her life and had never fully adjusted to the idea of living without them, even though it was much more convenient. A Lepidopteran's vestigial wings are far too heavy, always pulling at their back, and too awkwardly large, always knocking into things. Lee-a-lei's mechanical wings, in comparison, were much more compact and outfitted with all kinds of useful features like anti-grav generators. Also, they were bejeweled, glittery, and downright pretty... drawing attention away from Lee-a-lei's Lepidopteran biology which looked nightmarish and Kafkaesque to humans—the dominant species around this corner of space.

Am-lei would never voice her judgement of her mother's need for a prosthetic directly to her mother... the two of them were much too close for that. She wouldn't have wanted to hurt Lee-a-lei.

But Am-lei did judge her.

Even so, Am-lei knew it was a character flaw in herself to be so judgmental of her mother, so comparing her own self-criticism to her judgement of her mother was likely to jolt her into being a little kinder to herself. It was easier to be cruel to herself without noticing than to her mother.

Jeko stepped toward her bride and reached out with her trunk. With the finger-like tip of her trunk, she took hold of the edge of Am-lei's left wedding wing. She waved her trunk lightly, causing the gauzy fabric to billow ethereally. A smile twisted the mouth under her trunk.

Am-lei's proboscis uncurled and fluted a laugh that sounded like fairies singing in a magical meadow.

"That's better," Jeko said. "There's my butterfly."

Am-lei took a step toward Jeko too, closing the space between them, and wrapped her four long arms lightly around Jeko's solid girth, gently stroking and circling her talons against the puffier white fabric of her elephant's dress. Jeko's heart could almost burst every time Am-lei embraced her like that— the touch of her talons was so light, it was almost ticklish. It truly felt like the kind of amazing, unexpected blessing of having a wild butterfly land on you. Except it happened all the time, and Jeko couldn't believe how lucky she was.

"Everything is almost ready," Am-lei fluted. "The last thing is the bouquets, and Grandma Amy went to fetch them from the florist a few minutes ago. She was going to meet me here."

That meant they didn't have much time alone here before the ceremony. Regardless, Jeko dropped the fold of Am-lei's dress fabric she'd been holding and instead wrapped her trunk tightly around the insectoid's narrow shoulders, pulling her even closer.

Elephant and butterfly brides held each other, simply breathing and letting their hearts beat together in a moment that was only for them.

Then another knock came at the door, and without bothering to step away, Jeko trumpeted, "Come in." Usually she was shy about being physically affectionate with Am-lei when anyone else could see them, but today, it seemed silly to care.

The door cracked open, and an aged human face, lined with wrinkles, looked through the gap. Living on a human space station, both Jeko and Am-lei would have become well versed in human facial expressions even if neither of them had had a direct family member who was human. As it was, neither of them had the slightest trouble seeing the worried look on Grandma Amy's face.

"What's wrong?" Am-lei fluted.

"It's the flowers," Grandma Amy said. "There was a miscommunication, and the florist marked your wedding down as not happening for another week..."

Am-lei stiffened—a nifty trick given the innate stiffness of her exoskeleton. "So, they haven't finished growing," she fluted, dourly providing the logical conclusion.

"Yes, they're just sprouts. No actual flowers yet," Grandma Amy confirmed.

Am-lei and Jeko had selected flowers for their bouquets from the Crossroads Station gene bank which included genetic information for plants from hundreds of different worlds. They'd carefully chosen one type of flower from each world Jeko's parents had dragged her to before they'd finally settled down on Crossroads Station, so their bouquets would be a reflection of the journey that had ended with the two of them finally meeting, finally being brought together.

Both Am-lei and Grandma Amy—with their entirely different faces—managed to share the same stricken expression. On Am-lei it involved a tightly curled proboscis and the wriggling mouth parts at the base of the proboscis clenching like tiny fists. For Grandma Amy, it involved her human mouth straining and skewing, stretched tight across her face.

Jeko could easily read both of them, and their terror at the idea of something related to the wedding going wrong was hilarious to her. Her trunk shook with laughter which she couldn't hold back.

"Are you okay?" Am-lei's four talons grabbed ahold of Jeko supportively, as if she thought the elephant were having a breakdown.

But she was just laughing.

"I'm sorry," Jeko trumpeted when she'd recovered herself enough to choke out actual words. "You both looked so scared, like the station was going to explode and we all had to evacuate or something."

"But... your flowers..." Am-lei fluted. "They represented everywhere you've ever lived."

Jeko shrugged with both shoulders and trunk. "I live here now. And they're just flowers. I had fun picking them out with you, but if I don't have any flowers in my hands when we get married, it won't make us any less married."

"You're really not upset?" Am-lei pressed.

"When you plan something as complicated as a wedding, something's bound to go wrong," Jeko answered. "And as problems go, this is nothing."

Grandma Amy smiled. "I always liked you," she said. And Jeko knew that was true. Grandma Amy had always been especially nice to her when she and Am-lei had been children. That was part of why they'd decided to have a wedding ceremony modeled on the ones they'd seen in old Earth movies Grandma Amy had shown them as kids. They knew it would please her.

"It would still be nice to have flowers," Am-lei fluted, pensively.

Grandma Amy's smile widened. "Actually, I talked to the florist about that, and I got permission for you to pick flowers directly from the arboretum on the way to your ceremony. There's a field I can show you to, right next to the Karillow Glade where the ceremony's happening. And then you can have the flowers you originally ordered in a week, when they're ready."

"Sort of a one-week anniversary present, I guess," Am-lei fluted. "That's kind of nice."

"I've always wanted to pick flowers in the arboretum!" Jeko trumpeted. There were strict rules about harvesting the plants in the arboretum, and no matter how much she'd always wanted to curl her trunk around the stems of the flowers and snap off pretty buds, she had never dared break the rules. "We can really pick them?"

Grandma Amy nodded.

"It's like a wedding present from Crossroads Station itself!" Jeko proclaimed.

Grandma Amy walked with Jeko and Am-lei to the arboretum. The brides got a lot of admiring looks from station inhabitants they passed along the way. It's not every day you see an elephant and giant insect walking along, hand in hand, wearing fancy white gowns. Even on Crossroads Station, a place filled with dozens of different species including sentient plants and fish, they still made a rare, beautiful sight.

When they got to the arboretum—a hollow sphere in the middle of the spinning rings that composed Crossroads Station —the light from lanterns above the trees in the center of the sphere filtered down through the roof of leaves and dappled their white gowns with bright speckles of gold.

Grandma Amy led Jeko and Am-lei along a cobbled stone path to a field of flowers, open to the false sunlight from above.

"You can pick anything you want from here," she said. "Have fun, and I'll meet you in the Karillow Glade."

So, Jeko and Am-lei strolled through the field, under a sky composed of golden light and the far side of the arboretum, green, lush, and upside down from where they stood. Jeko picked pink, white, yellow, and purple blossoms. Am-lei gravitated towards only the white flowers that matched her fluttery false wings. To Jeko, she looked like an ethereal angel, and to Am-lei, her elphantine bride looked like a goddess of life and spring incarnate, plump, earthy, and brimming over with joy and love.

Jeko snapped the flowers off with her trunk and gathered them in her hands until her hands were full. "I think I have enough," she said. Though, part of her wanted to keep picking flowers in the golden light that wasn't quite sunlight and forget entirely about some silly little ceremony.

But their friends and family were waiting. And while she wanted to keep picking flowers, she also wanted to stand in front of all the people she cared about, beside her insectile angel, and proclaim their love. Time never stops passing, even when a moment is so perfect that you feel like you could live inside it forever.

"Let's go get married," Jeko said, accepting that it was time to let this perfect moment pass. There would be more perfect moments to come.

"Yes, let's," Am-lei agreed. She reached out a talon, and Jeko reached back, grasping the talon with the curled end of her trunk. They walked along together toward the ceremony awaiting them.

39

SKY RIVER

THE BLUE SUN of Lottie IV glinted off the watery world's ice rings. Rocky chunks of diamond gleamed with sapphire light, stretched in a crescent across the world's pale sky. Its inhabitants—a long-spined, thick-furred, water-breathing, lutrinae species—had stared at that crescent of glittering ice from Lottie's oceans for generations. Out of reach. Unconquerable.

Today the rings would be conquered.

Rockets had seeded their sky with outposts and space stations. Over the last six decades, less than a lifetime, the Lottians had schemed and plotted to claim their birthright in the ice that had taunted their ancestors' dreams.

Today the ice would melt.

And Brunaia had the honor of pushing the final button—big, round, and red. Everything it should be. The stuff of legends, wired into a control panel on a space station, waiting for her to lower her paw. Her claws brushed against the button's smooth surface, and Brunaia's fur prickled all down her long spine, to the very tip of her rudder-like tail, with anticipation and liminal excitement.

Voices buzzed over the space station's comm-system:

"The heaters are ready," reported the general in charge of the fleet of spaceships used to position heating coils at regular intervals around the ring.

"A sufficient surface area of the ice fragments have been sprayed with glu-factor," reported the general in charge of the drone-ships for spraying glu-factor.

"Everything is ready," Brunaia said, and her voice was carried to every Lottian in space around their world and most of the civilians planet-side. "Meltation now!" She pressed the button.

Heating coils buzzed to life and glowed a dull red, punctuating the arc of glittering diamonds that cut across the Lottian sky. For long moments, nothing else seemed to happen as the heating coils worked their magic, cutting into the ice. Frozen water boiled, molecules dancing away, captured by the vacuum of space. Then the glu-factor began to mix in, calming and soothing the frantic molecules, pulling them together with massive surface tension. Droplets held, clinging to the ice chunks like sweat, grabbing onto each other, until BLOOP. The melted water hit a critical mass and glommed into a planet-wide ring. A looping river in the sky.

Lottians cheered all over their world, splashing for joy, as they watched their arc of ice wobble into a flowing sickle of shimmery fluid. Ice chunks still floated inside the sky-river, but they would melt soon.

"Install the water-locks," Brunaia ordered, and the general in charge of the water-lock gates relayed the message to her teams. Mechanical water-locks pierced the surface tension of the ever-flowing river, evenly spaced between the heating coils. Lottians would be able to use them to enter the river.

Finally, Brunaia ordered, "Release the fish."

From every water-lock, brightly colored fish spilled into their new home. All the colors of the rainbow swam in a translucent arc across the sky.

Joy filled the Lottians' hearts.

Brunaia took a deep breath and said, "I declare the Rainbow River open."

The blue light of the sun shone through the river as Lottians launched from the water-locks, carrying armfuls of kelp that streamed out behind them like green pennants.

40

TRUE FEAST

ARGELNOX HUNCHED her shoulders inside her mechanical shell. The metal casing chafed against her soft, wrinkly green skin. She'd been traveling for months, solo-zipping from one planet to the next, skimming only deep enough into each planet's atmosphere to replenish her oxygen and basic nutrients, soaking them into her suit's mechanical gills before sling-shotting towards the next.

The purple-blue world beneath her was the last planet in this star-system. Once she left it behind, she'd fall into deep hibernation, solo-zipping through the deep space between here and the next star. The next palette of worlds to tickle her taste buds and tempt her. She shouldn't stop here; it would only slow her down, and she'd fallen far enough behind the migration.

Yet, the sun glowed orange over the purple rocky mountains in the distance, and her determination faltered. She dropped the power of her jets, letting herself fall into a descending orbit. Argelnox spiraled downward, the atmosphere burning against her metal shell. Wind whistled and roared against the clear dome shielding her oblong head; it was a glorious noise after months of only her own breathing echoed in her auditory canals.

Argelnox landed lightly on one of the purple mountaintops and descended the clear dome over her head backward into her mechanical shell, allowing the alien air and golden sunlight to bathe the naked green skin of her face. Her inner eyelids closed, slowly, luxuriously, as if she were preparing for a hundred year nap—the kind of nap that had left her behind the rest of the migration in the first place—but she didn't fall into hibernation this time.

She needed respite, but she needed to keep it short. Only a few days for searching out and collecting creepy crawlies among the purple rocks; a few more days to shed her mechanical shell and swim through the blue ocean, catching fish and jellies; then a week to say the prayers and perform the rites before finally settling down to a true feast.

She savored every bite taken with her chitinous beak—crunching the insects, chewing the jellies, and rolling the flaky fish over her tongue. It was all so much more revitalizing than a thin soup of gases absorbed through her mechanical shell. That could keep her alive, but this would keep her going.

When the feast was done, Argelnox ignited her rockets, blasted back through the atmosphere, and fell into the numbing rhythm of flying through space. She would catch up to her people eventually.

41

THE NIGHT JANITOR AND ALIEN OCEANS

RERIN JOSTLED the control panel while rubbing it down with a rag. The raccoon-like alien didn't know how the day-crew got the bridge controls so sticky. They were supposed to be searching the oceans on this world for signs of sentience—not snacking and boozing on Eridanii brandy. Rerin had expected janitorial detail on a starship full of human and s'rellick scientists to be an easy job. Instead, the naked-skinned primates partied all day, and the s'rellick shed scales everywhere—not to mention the extra work involved in tending to their live food. Ugh. Terrarium after terrarium filled with scuttling insects and rodents. Rerin would not be signing on with this ship again.

And yet, the view of the virgin planet they were studying was breathtaking. Framed by the bridge's broad curving windows, azure oceans were hugged by ragged dark wine-colored mountain ranges. It was the last planet in this star system, and each world had been more beautiful than the last—green swirling gas clouds on the first; the second had been entirely glittering ice; the third was another ocean world, but it had been studded with island chains like emerald gemstones.

None of them housed sentient life. At least, that's what the raucous human and s'rellick scientists had concluded. With the amount of Eridanii brandy they imbibed... Well, Rerin wasn't sure they could be trusted.

The raccoon-like alien finished scrubbing the sticky residue off of the pilot's controls, carefully avoiding bumping any of the glowing buttons or switches. She tucked the damp rag into her belt and knelt down to gather up the empty glass bottles discarded under the communications console. Her ringed tail swayed with agitation as she strained to reach far enough with her black-furred paw.

"Ouch!" Rerin exclaimed, cutting her paw on a piece of broken glass. Startled by the pain, she wasn't careful in pulling her arm out. Rerin stumbled and fell against the control panel, pressing heaven knows how many buttons and catching her rag on one of the switches. "No, no, no..." She held her paws out, wanting to fix it, but she had no idea which buttons had been green before and were red now. One of them was even yellow. Had any of them been yellow before?

Rerin held her injured paw to her mouth; the black fur was matted with blood. She was still trying to figure out what to do —whether she had to tell the scientists about her blunder or not—when the computer said in a mechanical voice, "Receiving transmission. Translation 80% complete. Please wait."

Rerin's rounded ears flattened, and she looked out the window at those oceans again. Was there someone down there? Someone sending a message into orbit?

"Translation complete," the computer intoned. "Play now?"

"Uh... sure," Rerin answered.

"Begin message: *Hello? Hello? I've been scanning the skies and picked up your burst of radio waves just now. Welcome to Oceanica! No one is going to believe me that I've found signs of extra-oceanic life in orbit of our very own planet! Please don't leave without answering me. I'm going to transmit several image files now—I hope you can decrypt them!* End message." After a few moments, the computer added, "Image files decrypted. Display now?"

"Yes, please!" Rerin exclaimed, whiskers quivering with excitement.

The computer screen over the communication array flickered to life, showing several images of a whale-like creature, grinning widely, mouth filled with shaggy baleen. Its flippers were divided into wedge-like fingers, and its long tail curled under it with a surprising flexibility as it floated beside some sort of computer console. Its small eyes sparkled.

The delight in the alien whale's expression was infectious.

Rerin knew she should alert the scientists onboard immediately, but she let herself get caught up in the whale's friendly demeanor anyway. "Send a return message," Rerin said to the computer. "Begin message: Hello back! Thank you for the images. The vessel orbiting your world is a science ship, searching for sentient life. I guess we found it! I'm actually the night janitor... But I'm really excited to meet you. End message." After a moment's thought, Rerin added, "Computer, can you transmit the image file of the profile picture for crewmember Rerin?"

"Affirmative," the computer answered. "Transmitting." Lights twinkled on the communications console. "Return message received. Begin message: you're a land mammal! I didn't know that was possible. Can you come down to visit? Can you teach us to build starships of our own? End message."

Rerin's rounded ears splayed. She realized that she was getting in past her depth. She didn't know the answers to those questions—or probably any of the other questions this alien whale would have. It was probably time to turn this conversation over to the experts who were actually prepared.

Still, she decided to send one more message. "Computer, begin message: Like I said, I'm only the night janitor, so I'm going to go wake up the scientists who you really want to talk to... But can I ask you for one thing first?"

The alien whale responded, "Anything!"

Rerin had sworn to herself that she was done with this ship as soon as they hit the next space station... But now that she'd seen the wonder of discovering an alien race firsthand, she wasn't so sure. Still, she deserved more respect than the humans and s'rellick scientists gave her.

"Tell the scientists that their janitor needs a raise!" Somehow, Rerin figured the request would carry more weight coming from a newly encountered cetacean alien.

42

SOMEWHERE OVER THE OCEAN

A'LOO'LOO SWAM eagerly back and forth, impatient for the spaceship above her, floating on the ocean's surface, to open its hatchway. There had been so little warning—A'loo'loo had only discovered the burst of radio waves coming from her planet's orbit three tides ago. Everything had changed since then.

The inhabitants of Oceanica were not alone in the universe, and the aliens who had come to them from the void above the sky were strange. They breathed the thin gases that floated above the true world, rather than good, nourishing water. A'loo'loo's own people had evolved out of a dependence on breathing those wispy gases through their vestigial blowholes millennia ago.

The hatchway of the spaceship opened, and three aliens emerged, each of them wearing a breathing mask over their face. One had green scales; another was covered with fuzzy grey-and-black fur; and the final one had appropriately smooth skin, except for a strange long mane sprouting from its head. All of them had bizarrely brachiated bodies—four primary limbs and weirdly narrow, weak tails that would serve as very poor rudders. Except for the smooth-skinned one—it had no tail at all! All three flailed about pathetically.

A'loo'loo wondered if they moved more gracefully in the thin gaseous atmosphere they were used to.

The waters shifted around A'loo'loo, and she looked over to see that the Senatorial Master had glided up beside her.

"Your visitors from above are not very impressive." The Senatorial Master's voice was low and fluting.

A'loo'loo hoped that the aliens' computer translators had missed the snide remark. She risked rebuking her leader: "They came here from an entirely different ocean—across the void above the thin gases. That is not impressive?"

The Senatorial Master waved one flipper and then the other, rocking back and forth in a shrug. A perfect demonstration of the scientific indifference that had nearly defunded A'loo'loo's international telescope three times. It was a wonder she'd had the tools to contact these alien visitors at all.

"Testing... Testing... Can you hear me?" The artificial-sounding voice emanated from the green-scaly alien.

A'loo'loo flipped her powerful blue tail in delight. "Yes!" she sang out. "Welcome to Oceanica! This is our Senatorial Master —" she pointed a flipper at him, "—and I'm the scientist you were talking with before. Are you ready for a tour of our fine capital city?"

The Senatorial Master snorted through his baleen. He was clearly picturing how long it would take to escort these awkward creatures about. "Tell you what," he said. "Take your time on the tour. A feast is prepared in your honor in the senate chambers—I'll see you all there."

With that, the Senatorial Master turned tail and left a wake of roiling water behind him, wasting no time in escaping from his diplomatic duties.

"My sincere apologies," A'loo'loo said to the three aliens. "I cannot convince my people that your visit is anything more than an oddity. Very few of them understand the vast difference between leaving our ocean for the thin atmosphere that surrounds it, and actually ascending all the way to the void above and crossing to an entirely different sphere of oceans." With great shame, A'loo'loo admitted, "Some of them do not even believe there are other spheres of ocean."

The three aliens assured A'loo'loo with their artificial voices that each of their worlds had gone through similar phases before developing spacefaring technology. Comforted, A'loo'loo encouraged each of them to take hold of her flippers, and she swam them down in a wide spiral that showed off the capital city from every angle. They admired the coral statues, grown into the shapes of heroic Oceanicans of yore, and politely complimented A'loo'loo's personal pride and joy—the great library filled with kelp-scrolls, containing all the knowledge her culture had attained.

From talking to the aliens, though, A'loo'loo had a sneaking suspicion that the computers they talked about contained far more information than all the kelp-scrolls put together. She wondered if their praise would sound condescending if it weren't filtered through artificial, translated voices.

At the end of the tour, a crew of cetacean ballerinas performed in the senatorial chambers for the visiting aliens. They twirled and somersaulted and swam in formation; the dance ended with two of them ceremonially ripping open the woven nets of krill and baby shrimp, delicate jellyfish and delectable fetal crabs. The colorful feast exploded outward, and every Oceanican in the room inhaled deeply through their baleen, swallowing gullets-full of the delicious morsels.

The scaly-green alien plucked a few fetal crabs from the swell and popped them under its breathing mask to munch on them. The smooth-skinned alien and the fuzzy ring-tailed one abstained, earning another derisive snort from the Senatorial Master.

After the floating feast cleared from the water, a cetacean poet performed a bubbly recitation. Then the Senatorial Master gave a disturbingly insular speech about the singular greatness of Oceanica.

A'loo'loo found herself tiring of her own species' pompous presentations and itching to hear more from the visitors about the other oceans they'd visited.

Alas, before she could plead with them to tell her stories about the worlds beyond the void, the scaly-green one announced, "Our oxygen filters are nearly worn out. We must return to our ship."

With a growing sense of urgency, afraid she was losing opportunities moment by moment, A'loo'loo complied to swim the visitors back up to their vessel, floating on the surface of her world.

Along the way, A'loo'loo asked, "Will you come visit again?"

The smooth-skinned alien replied, "We have enough material from this single visit to write many papers. I'm sure other scientists will come, but it may be a long time before they do."

"Will you give us the information we'd need to follow you into the void?"

The scaly-green one answered, "You don't have any technology that can download our computer banks... Besides, it will take your species generations—at least—to build the infrastructure necessary to support space travel."

Regretfully, A'loo'loo arrived at the underside of the aliens' spaceship and asked one final question: "Will you take me with you?"

The fuzzy ring-tailed one, who was the first of the aliens to have talked to A'loo'loo over the radio waves, said, "Trapped in a fish tank? I don't think so. There's nowhere on our ship that you'd be comfortable."

If underwater species cried, then A'loo'loo's bright eyes would have filled with tears.

"However," the scaly-green one offered, "now that we know you're here, perhaps a spacefaring race of water-breathers will take an interest in reaching out to you. The Lintar are always looking to expand their trade routes."

"Keep your eyes on the sky," the smooth-skinned one added.

As if A'loo'loo would ever stop watching the sky, now that she knew what out-of-reach wonders filled it.

43

TREASURE IN THE SKY

THE SHORT, stout, furry alien stared out the starship's curving bridge window at the star-studded black sky. His black fur blended into the sky like a shadow, but the blaze of white over his forehead stood out like a brand. His rounded ears splayed, and he curled his heavy claws into fists. "I don't belong here," he muttered, and the ship's computer translated it. "None of my people do."

The human and s'rellick scientists—smooth-skinned primatoids and scaly-green reptilians, respectively—conferred among themselves and then agreed to take the badger-like alien home to the surface of his world.

"Thank you," the badger-like alien said, bowing his fuzzy head. Then he backed away from the yawning window, as if it were a portal that he could fall through and never land, floating forever, lost in the void of space. He backed into the nearest hallway and pressed his back against the firm wall, feeling its comforting solidity like an anchor.

Rerin watched him, wondering how the s'rellick and human scientists looked to him. Esoteric. Lofty. Out of touch. Strange scaly and naked gods of the sky. They seemed that way to her sometimes. She wasn't one of them. She was the ship's janitor—and, at least at a superficial level, she ought to look more familiar to the badger-like alien: black-and-gray fur, a fluffy ring-striped tail, and curved ears that showed her emotions in how they moved.

Right now, Rerin's ears were perked forward with interest and curiosity. When she'd joined this mission, she'd expected the sentient races that the scientists discovered on their survey to be more excited by first contact with the outside universe. Instead, many of them were afraid, confused, or simply uninterested.

Rerin reached a paw out to the badger-like alien and rested it on his shoulder. He looked around to see her, and relief filled his shiny eyes. "It's not only lizards and monkeys up here?" he said.

"There are all kinds of species up here," Rerin said. "Even fish that fill their spaceships with water to breathe."

The badger-like alien's eyes twinkled with what seemed like laughter, but then he turned serious again. "That's a relief. I was afraid..." He trailed off.

Rerin suspected that he didn't even know what he was afraid of. Simply, his world had turned upside down in the last week, and suddenly the sky was filled with a larger, more powerful network of beings than lived in the tunnels and subterranean kingdoms of his home.

"Don't give up on space," Rerin said. "You may not feel like you belong up here, but there are wonders..." Now she trailed off, thinking about the disparate alien species who lived side-by-side on Crossroads Station and the glittering virgin worlds she'd seen on this ship as they searched for previously undiscovered sentient life. Her ring-striped tail swayed lazily from side to side as she lost herself in beautiful memories. "...so many wonders..."

"Treasure in the sky," the badger-like alien said.

"Yes," Rerin agreed, a grin splitting her fuzzy muzzle. She might be only the night janitor on this ship, but it still felt like she was on a voyage to collect treasure from where it had been hidden among the stars.

"I'll try to convince my people to see it that way," the badger-like alien said. "And maybe someday we'll be comfortable joining you up here."

But not today. Today, he intended to return to the safe warrens and splendid grottoes under the mountains on a world that had suddenly become small. There was treasure on his own world too, and for now, that was enough for him.

Let the treasure in the sky be a seed. Someday, it might bloom. For now, let it sleep above the mountains.

44

TOO MANY JANGLEBERRIES

Franzi swung her long, giraffe-like neck from side to side, surveying the tightly filled shelves of the grocery aisles on this asteroid shop-mart. There were too many brands of jangleberries to pick from—she didn't know which kind she'd like best, and somehow, the existence of so many brands made her feel like she shouldn't have to settle for anything less than her absolute favorite type of jangleberry.

It had been a long day for Franzi. It had been a long cycle. Her latest trip between the art district in Sinuria's ice rings and the market district under the uppermost layer of Jortan's gas clouds had drained her more than she'd let on to the rest of her crew.

And right now, all she wanted was a taste of jangleberries—sweet and sour on the tip of her tongue. She felt like it would be enough to rejuvenate her. Enough to give her energy to lead her crew onward, get the art they'd picked up sold at a profit, and maybe get out of this racket forever. She didn't want to be a mercenary—a middleman. She wanted to be an artist herself, but the artist residency program in Sinuria's ice rings would always be too expensive for her. She'd have to settle for being an artist somewhere less picturesque than surrounded by glittering balls of ice, circling above a beautiful sea-green ocean world.

That was okay. She didn't mind settling. But not this much—not all the way down to being a middleman instead of an artist herself.

Franzi reached out with a hoof-hand toward the closest jar of jangleberries, and as the rough tips of her keratinous fingers brushed the glass holding the ripe, red berries, she felt a fracture in her world.

A single sub-atomic particle rattled, shifting its orbit, and for a moment, Franzi felt her consciousness split across time, or maybe universes... She wasn't sure.

She stood perfectly still; yet her whole body shook, from the bottom of her long legs up to the tips of her conical ears. She felt a tingling in the ossicones atop her head, and she saw too many images with her eyes, all of them superimposed upon each other. She shouldn't have been able to tell them apart, but somehow, she could.

In one universe, she took the jar of jangleberries, opened it immediately without buying it, and dipped her prehensile tongue into the morass of juicy balls of fruit, only to find them too sour. She spat them out and dashed the glass jar angrily upon the floor.

In another universe—or maybe just an imagined universe—she held the closed jar close to her face, peered at the tiny print, and carefully considered the listed ingredients before concluding this brand used too much Zevusian vinegar and putting the jar back.

Those were just the closest universes.

Farther and farther out, her mind stretched, like an accordion played by an overly enthusiastic child, or like the images in two mirrors pointed directly at each other. The farther her mind slipped through the universes, the stranger everything got:

Dozens of short arms sprouted from either side of her neck, each one reaching for a different jangleberry jar. As her mind slipped into that universe, suddenly, all the extra arms didn't feel strange—didn't feel extra—they were simply how she'd always been.

In another moment, her consciousness slipped into a reality where her whole body was covered in thick, plated armoring. She'd shifted from being a giraffe crossed with a centipede into being a giraffe crossed with an armadillo, and she only knew what those creatures were because—in yet another reality— she became a smooth-skinned primate with a funny, flat yet knobby face, and hair growing only from the top of her head.

Wait, she wondered, *am I truly a human dreaming of being a bizarre alien giraffe, shopping for groceries in an asteroid belt? Or am I the giraffe, dreaming of being a human?*

Or were they both the dream?

A giraffe, dreaming of a human, dreaming of a giraffe, dreaming of a human, and on and on, forever, until the universe was filled with giraffes and humans, uncertain of how they related to each other.

A sharp cry came from the front of the store—a voice Franzi recognized as one of her crewmembers, probably fighting with a grocery clerk, insisting on being given a line of credit when both knew full well their ship wouldn't be back by this asteroid again for months. If ever.

The moment of self-reflecting eternities ended, and Franzi found herself still standing—fingertips resting on the glass jangleberry jar—filled with a sense of possibility.

And yet, even with seeing all those realities and all the possible and bizarre ways her life could be...

She still didn't know which brand of jangleberries to buy.

45

MOON DUST

Rainal gripped the vial of moon dust tightly in her clawed hand. It was the only vial she had left. Without it... No, she wouldn't think about that. She would find a new source of dust in this space station bazaar. Someone had to be selling it.

Rainal passed one shop after another: avian aliens with fearsome hooked beaks and massive talons sold specially tailored clothing; reptilian aliens with scaly hides that gleamed like finely polished armor sold tech upgrades for starhoppers; and ursine aliens that towered over everyone with their impressive furry bulk sold dishes of curry.

Rainal wouldn't want to face any one them in her natural form. Without her moon dust. Even in her were-form, she felt like her claws were too small, her muzzle too cute, her teeth too demure. None of these aliens would fear or respect her naked-skinned, flat-toothed human form. She needed moon dust to protect herself. She needed moon dust to stay lupine.

"Excuse me," Rainal barked with a flash of her sharp teeth. An alien with bright orange fur, long curling antennae, and multi-faceted eyes stopped to listen. "Do you know—is there an apothecary shop near here?"

The bright orange alien's antennae unfurled, trembled and vibrated, then curled back up again. The alien buzzed, "There's a Klai who deals in potions and rare minerals up ahead." The bright orange alien pointed with a many-jointed arm.

Rainal thanked the alien, who was upsettingly similar to a gigantic bee, and hurried through the crowds. As Rainal darted between fearsome aliens of all stripes, her own gray-furred tail swished eagerly, hopefully behind her.

The apothecary shop had a glass window, and several geodes larger than Rainal's head were on display. Their cracked-open innards sparkled with crystals. Brushes of sage-green leaves with tiny violet flowers hung, drying from above. Rainal rushed inside. Little bells rang on the door as it swung open and then shut behind her.

The werewolf perused the shelves, tapping stones with her claws in hopes that they'd vibrate with that special tingly resonance. She unstoppered vials, sniffed the dust inside them, and sighed when it smelled flat and musty with none of the strangely citrusy zing she was seeking.

"Can I help you?" a voice asked from behind.

Rainal whirled about in surprise, dropping her own vial. The glass cracked, and precious moon dust spilled out on the floor. "No!" Rainal cried, kneeling down. She clawed at the shimmery dust, trying to sweep it into a savable pile. Her paws grew shaggier and her claws sharper at the touch of the dust.

"Here, let me," the voice said.

A pair of keratinous hoof-hands gently pushed Rainal's shaggy paws aside, slipped a thin piece of paper under the dust, and then carefully poured it into a new, unbroken vial.

Rainal looked up to see a pair of doe-brown eyes staring at her from a long, fuzzy-brown, speckled face. Conical ears flipped fore and back at the top of the creature's head in a nervous dance. This was the most unintimidating alien that Rainal had ever seen.

"Are you the Klai?" Rainal asked.

The deer-like creature answered, "Yes, my name is Orri."

At least, this explained to Rainal how the Klai had sneaked up on her. In her werewolf form, very little escaped her sensitive, pointed ears. But this alien was a prey-based creature, designed for camouflage and stealth from those adorable speckles on her fur to the careful way she moved her long, slender limbs.

Rainal felt a quickening in her heart. She wasn't sure if she felt excited by the presence of a creature weaker than her—someone that her sharp teeth and claws could rend to pieces—or by the presence of a creature similar to her, one who seemed fearful and hiding. Like Rainal felt, in spite of her bushy gray fur and sharp teeth and claws.

This was a chance for true connection, unlike anything she'd felt since fleeing Earth in her little starhopper. Rainal had hoped to escape her curse by getting as far away as possible from the lunar body that caused it—and the people who feared her when she changed. Instead, she found herself clinging to the curse in this bizarre universe of terrifying aliens. She missed her home, but at home she was a monster. Anyone who differed was a monster.

Out here, she was surrounded by monsters. And they were all different from each other. She didn't know how to fit in.

"I'll have to charge you for the replacement vial," Orri said. "But I've never seen dust like this before, so I'd be willing to take my fee in the form of a small sample."

"No!" Rainal barked again, grabbing the vial from Orri's hoofish hands. Perhaps Rainal didn't have to be a monster out here to fit in—but she was afraid not to be.

"It must be very valuable, for you to treasure it so." Orri didn't flinch, in spite of Rainal's sudden viciousness.

Why wasn't she afraid?

"Where did you get it?" Orri pressed.

Rainal felt her fur thinning, her shoulders narrowing, and her muzzle shortening. She was growing less fearsome by the moment. More human. More weak. More vulnerable. "It's from the moon of the planet I came from. I can't go back there. The government doesn't tolerate people like me. People who change. They set up a ring of space-drones to shoot me down if I come back. They think I'll infect others. But I need more dust to live out here."

"You're a lycanthrope," Orri said.

Rainal touched her face in a panic, but her muzzle was still there. She looked at her paws—they were still paws, not hands. She was still in her lupine form, even if she was turning into a weak, scraggly werewolf.

"Are you afraid of your alternate form?" Orri asked. "What do you turn into?"

"A naked primate," Rainal answered, flooded with shame and the rush of intimacy at the confession.

"We don't get a lot of primatoid species here."

"No kidding," Rainal barked. "You're the first creature I've seen without massive claws and teeth or a giant stinger on its butt since I started starhopping."

Orri laughed. Her doe-brown eyes crinkled from her smile, and her voice sounded like tinkling bells. "They do look scary, don't they?"

"Aren't they?"

"Are you?"

Rainal blinked her yellow eyes. They'd turn back to blue soon, if she didn't sprinkle moon dust over herself. "I don't always know. People told me I was scary. I started to believe them. But sometime I wonder if I was just different."

Orri held out a keratinous hoof-hand and waited patiently until Rainal took hold of it with her furry—no longer shaggy— paw. "I don't think you're scary," Orri said.

Rainal's fingers grew longer, and her claws rounded into

nails. Orri clasped her rough hoofish fingers tightly around Rainal's as her werewolf paw reformed itself into a human hand.

When the transformation was complete, Rainal's clothes hung loosely on her human body, no longer needing the extra space for fur. She knelt on the floor beside Orri, hand in hooves. Human girl and deer-like alien.

"When I'm not scary," Rainal whispered, thinking of all the fearsome aliens just outside the apothecary shop, "I'm afraid."

Orri squeezed her hand. "Freedom feels a lot like fear, when you're not used to it. You'll get used to it. Then it won't be so bad."

Rainal tilted the vial in her other hand and watched the moon dust shimmer. It wasn't enough left for her to stay a werewolf all the time, but it would last much longer if she only used it occasionally. Only when she wanted the rush of living inside her other form. Rather than a shield to protect herself all the time.

"Can you tell me about the other aliens?" Rainal asked, her human voice quavering. "You live here; you must know about them." Maybe the giant bees and bears and dragon-like reptiles would be less scary if she knew more about them. Maybe she was only afraid of them because all the humans back home had trained her to be afraid of anything that was different.

"I have some stock to rearrange in the back," Orri said, rising on her slender legs. "Help me, and we can talk while we work."

"Thank you," Rainal said, following the deer-like woman toward the back of her apothecary shop. "I'd like that."

46

TREASURE MOON

ALARM BELLS RANG out and lights flashed red from the corners of the buildings on either side of the street. A mechanical turret rising out of the middle of the mountaintop base swung around and cast invisible laser beams, searching for the intruder, but Rikkita threw herself to the ground and spread her wide, bushy tail over her back. The fur on her tail was ultra-dark black; it would confuse the algorithms processing the data from the lasers. As long as she held still, she was safe.

The alarms were only an automated safety system. There were no sentient guards here, neither biological nor robotic. At least, that's what Rikkita's intel suggested. Of course, her intel also gave her an access code that blew this whole place wide with blaring, screaming alarms.

Rikkita's small pointed ears flattened against her head, trying to shut out the screech of the alarms. It would all be over soon, and she'd crack that door code the old-fashioned way.

A few deep breaths later, the mountaintop base fell eerily silent. Rikkita peeked out from under her wide tail. Everything was dark again. Perfect. She skittered back over to the door into her cousin Alvo's hidden headquarters. She reached a paw into her pocket, pulled out an antiquated computer pad, and hot-wired it into the door's access panel. The antique software on the computer pad set up a protected shell where Rikkita could test different passcodes without fully entering them into the system.

First, she tried the name of the planet where her cousin and all the rest of their family used to meet up on vacations—a world called Lottie III, whose aquatic otter-like inhabitants had built the best waterparks in the Western Spiral Arm of the galaxy. Alvo had been happier on those vacations than anytime else. But it was not the password.

She tried the names of each of Cousin Alvo's pets from their kithood—Qui'Laia the dragonfish; On'no'ni the tapestry-spider; and George the creature he'd bought from a human merchant. The human had called it a squirrel, and it was damn creepy. It had looked like a miniature sub-sentient version of Alvo, and everyone in the family was relieved when it had died.

None of the pet names worked, but thinking about George reminded Rikkita of Alvo's favorite game from back then. The human merchant had told him that squirrels collected and hoarded acorns. So, Alvo had created a game where all the cousins collected and hoarded treasures—little plastic baubles, trading cards, costume jewelry—and called it "Acorn."

That password worked. Rikkita unhooked the computer pad and input the code directly into the door. It swung open on its mechanical hinges. Lights on the inside turned on automatically, welcoming Rikkita into her cousin's abandoned lair.

Rikkita entered the room, taking slow cautious steps.

"Welcome to the treasure trove!" A flickering blue hologram of Alvo spread his arms wide, as if he were surrounded by piles of gold. But it was just a small room with plain walls and a tacky paisley-patterned carpet.

"This is a recording, isn't it?" Rikkita asked.

The hologram of Alvo twitched his wide bushy tail. "If

you've located this dwarf moon in an uninhabited solar system, made it past the drone ships in the moon's orbit, located my mountaintop base, and infiltrated the base's defenses all the way to my headquarters, then you're either very clever or one of my cousins." The hologram flashed a bucktoothed grin. "Or both! Hi, Rikkita."

Rikkita laughed in spite of herself. "This was all just a big game of Acorn to you, wasn't it?" She shook her head. "And you're still just a recording."

"Actually," the hologram said, surprising her. "I'm an interactive AI set up by your cousin, Alvo, to mimic his own behavior."

Rikkita was furious—her cousin had disappeared on the family, leaving a trail of clues through half a dozen starsystems. She'd been chasing him down for years, ever since Aunt Ido took sick. Alvo's connections would buy her better care; with attention from the scientists at Wespirtech, Ido could be cured instead of merely treated, managing symptoms and slowly wasting away.

Still, the idea that Alvo had been playing a kit's game with her all along tickled Rikkita, and her tail flipped happily. Now that she was here, her cousin would finally listen to reason and come back to the family.

"Your mother's sick," Rikkita said.

The blue hologram skewed with a burst of static, and then Alvo said, "I don't have a programmed response for that."

"Dammit, Alvo!" Rikkita swore.

"In the hangar on the far side of the base," the AI of Alvo continued, ignoring her outburst, "you will find a spaceship programmed with the initial clues for the next leg of your journey!"

Rikkita muttered under her breath, "I can't keep chasing you forever."

"It's stocked with all the supplies that you'll need. Of course, if you'd rather, you'll find that this mountaintop base is stocked with enough treasure to make you very comfortable and fund whichever adventures you'd prefer to pursue."

Rikkita skewed one ear, giving the hologram a sidelong look. "You always were a weird one, Alvo." She pulled a blaster out of her belt and shot the holo-generator in the ceiling of the room. "I will take that ship, and whatever treasure fits on it."

Now that she was inside the base's headquarters, it was easy to shut down the alarm systems. Rikkita spent several days hauling the easiest to liquidate treasures—rare mineral composites, precious energy crystals, and ultra-fast computer processors—into the cargo hold of the ship Alvo had left for her. She left the buildings full of ancient cultural artifacts from across the spiral arm, stolen art, and stacks upon stacks of hard-copy of secrets gathered from high level officials at all the biggest starbases alone. She wasn't interested in dealing in blackmail.

When the ship was all loaded, Rikkita reengaged the base's security systems. Who knew, maybe she'd come back some day.

As she flew away from Alvo's treasure moon, Rikkita found herself studying her new ship's computer banks, looking for Alvo's clues. Sure, she had obligations right now. But once Aunt Ido was set up with the Wespirtech doctors, and the rest of the family was properly cared for with the rest of this load of trea-sure... Well, someone would need to find Alvo and tell him how his mother was doing.

Besides, Rikkita wanted to know what other surprises Alvo had waiting for her in this epic game of Acorn.

47

THIRTY HONEY FEASTS TO GO

MARGA HELD her broad paw up to the star-studded window, lining it up so a single spark of light tipped each of her blunted claws. Her own constellation. She wondered if any of those stars had habitable worlds circling them. She knew none of them was New Sholara. Not from this window. Not from this side of the ship.

A purple-and-amber-striped worker bee buzzed down and landed on the thick brown fur of Marga's shoulder, reminding her that life support was limited. She left the window behind and moved from one cryonics pod to the next, starting their rejuv cycles. Bees followed her, buzzing in the air.

"How many Honey Feasts are left?" Marga rumbled.

The electronic voice of the ship's computer answered, "Thirty, maybe forty."

"And how many generations of queens have passed since the last feast?"

"My great-great-great-grandmother was the last queen who had the honor of awakening you," the ship's computer answered. It was a hybrid brain—part computer, part hive—with the reigning bee queen at its heart.

The blue lights on the cryonics pods flashed and turned green, one at a time, and sleepy ursines emerged, fur rumpled and jaws wide with yawns. The elders woke first; Marga saved the rows and rows of cubs for last.

Some of the cubs were young enough they'd known nothing but Honey Feasts. Day after day of Honey Feasts, each one followed by a long nap, many light-years long, as the sleeper ship hurtled through the universe, bringing them all closer to their new home.

The cubs roared and scuffled and chased the busy bees while the older ursines laid silky sheets over the emptied cryonics pods, turning them into picnic tables. Worker bees carried dripping, golden chunks of honey comb through the air and set them on the tables. All the extra honey they'd made during their last five generations, carefully saved for this Honey Feast.

For the first fifty Honey Feasts, the supper tables had been filled with boisterous conversation, excited speculation, and so much planning. After a hundred or so—Marga had lost count —the adults mostly ate their nutrient-enriched honey in silence, except for the occasional, nearly ritual, exchange:

"The stars look different."

"We haven't flown far enough for them to be different; these are the same constellations we saw on Old Sholara."

"Maybe it's just the weight of experience, changing my eyes."

Or:

"The cubs don't appreciate what we're doing for them."

"They don't remember the arachnoid wars."

"Would you want them to?"

After all the bellies were full, maws and paws sticky, the ursines felt a restless stirring, but there was no way to spend the energy here. There was only time for bedtime stories for the cubs—half their lives had been bedtime stories—and the sense of relief when their boundless energy was again bottled in cryonics pods, cradled through the eons that passed on this ship of buzzing halls.

Marga was the last ursine awake, as always. She climbed into her cryonics pod, but before lying down, she said, "Tell me again, how many Honey Feasts to go?"

The amber and purple striped bees swarmed around her pod, working together to lift the hinged lid and close her in safely for her hibernation. Through their roaring buzz, Marga heard the computer-queen tell her the same thing she said every time, "It won't be long now. Hush now, dear, and go to sleep."

"Can you see New Sholara? Does it look bigger?" Marga asked the question too late, already sealed in her somnolent shell, but she dreamed of a yellow sun and a blue-green world, glittering with water and land, ready for cub paws to dance on its virgin dirt.

48

THE UNIFICATION OF WORLDS

Diamma's scaly green tail curled to one side, then the other, swaying uneasily, as she stood in the open hatch of her spaceship. Crystals of pink snow caught in her fiery, leonine mane as the flakes drifted down from the powder blue clouds of this world. Snomoth. For years, it had been a number in the registry on her ship; somewhere she would eventually go. For the last few weeks, it had been a dot of light on the main viewscreen. Now it was a faintly pink snowball, the color of cherry blossoms in the early spring, stretched out before her, waiting to freeze her toes when she stepped down from the hatch.

The final piece of the puzzle might be here, hidden underneath the pale pink snow.

The feline-reptilian hybrid stepped into the snow, and the crunching crystalline drift burned cold on the pawpads of her tawny-tufted feet. It made her wish that her green armor of shimmering scales extended all the way to her hind feet, instead of only from her taloned-hands down to her haunches, leaving her with a lion's hind paws and a lion's head.

Better yet, Diamma wished for hooves like Aggem, her

antlered-avian co-pilot. Or elephant feet like Mundo, the turtle-shelled, prehensile-nosed, painfully pedantic researcher who led their team. Aggem and Mundo were both busy inside the spaceship, studying the genetic blueprints their team had assembled from the many dozens of worlds they'd visited so far. There was always more studying to be done.

Diamma's paw pads adjusted to the burn of the cold as she loped her way through the snow with an easy hind-legged gait, balancing herself with a rhythmic sway of her long scaly tail. The ship's scans had shown architectural structures only a few kilometers away. A short run. They'd landed far enough away to be out of sight, but only from a society that wasn't looking at the skies.

The skies here were shrouded in permanent layers of cloud —the powder blue clouds sprinkling Diamma with snow crystals were only the bottom layer. Snomoth's blue giant sun was bright enough to glow through the clouds, but dimly. Diamma's feline eyes were the best suited in her crew to handle the low light levels.

As Diamma ran through the snow, she passed by scrub brushes and waist-high bushes with yellow and topaz leaves. The plants thickened into a veritable forest of tiny shrubbery for her to dart and dodge around. Then Diamma crested a slight rise, not steep enough for her to have recognized it was a hill until she was on the top of it, and she saw the city from the ship's scans in the distance.

The buildings were tiny—the tallest skyscrapers were maybe two- or three-times Diamma's height. Most of them were ankle high. They all had rounded edges and oval windows, some of which glowed with light from inside. They were all frosted with the pink snow. Between the buildings, tiny mechanical sledges skated along the icy streets, lit by sparkling street lights.

The creatures who rode inside the sledges and scurried

from one building to another were small enough to fit in the palm of one of Diamma's scaly hands. Their pastel fur looked thick, but they wore bulky winter coats anyway. Their ears were large and round; their tails long and skinny with big puffs of fur on the end.

"Another mouse-like species," Diamma muttered to herself, wondering what genetic quirk of these Snomoth mice could be so special that the project was incomplete without them.

Mundo's nasal voice spoke into the receiver in her ear. The elephant-turtle hybrid said, "It's not about being special. It's about being a piece of the puzzle." He'd heard her talking to herself, but he knew her well enough, it was as if he'd heard her thinking too.

The lion-lizard hybrid settled onto her leonine haunches and watched the alien mice scurry through their snowy streets. Their sudden, tiny movements as they unloaded from the sledges or carried parcels across the streets made Diamma's heart jump and race, triggering predatory genes from both the reptilian and feline halves of her ancestral genetics. At a deep level, before civilization, before star-faring space travel, she was meant to hunt creatures like this.

And she was still hunting them. And they would still be consumed—but not by her. She was only the hunter.

Diamma waited patiently while the glowing light from the clouds above deepened to azure and then darkened to midnight blue; window lights twinkled out in the tiny city below. It was the snow-mice's night time. The lion-lizard perched over their city like a green-and-gold albatross, signifying the end of times, removed a syringe with a long needle from a pouch at her waist. She tapped the glass with one of her scaly talons, and it pinged softly. All she needed was a sample of blood.

Bright light shone into Diamma's eyes, and she raised her empty talon to block it. The light came from the ground in a single piercing beam. A flashlight. In the shaking paws of a quivering Snomoth mouse with buttercup-yellow fur. The creature squeaked in the common language of the stars, "You're the Unifier of Worlds."

Diamma's feline heart was pleased by the mouse's recognition. "Your legends tell of me, even though your world cut itself off from the intergalactic highways millennia ago."

"You're why we cut ourselves off," the mouse answered, still quivering, still shining the flashlight at Diamma's leonine face. Snow sparkled in the bright beam of light.

"Put down the light," Diamma purred.

The beam lowered. Then clicked off.

"Hold very still," she purred, lifting the syringe. She wouldn't have to catch a mouse; one had come to her.

"Wait," the mouse squeaked. "Take me with you. The universe is ending; take me with you!"

Diamma hesitated. "We don't know that the universe will end. We don't even know that your blood holds the final piece of the puzzle."

"But Snomoth is the last world on your itinerary, isn't it?" the mouse insisted. "We've always known we were last." The mouse's wide ears splayed, spilling pink snow crystals that had piled on them.

Diamma shook her mane, raining down more snow that had caught in her thick fur. "All I need is a drop of your blood; your genetic code. Your life here can go on as normal. Whatever happens when we complete the unification could take years, lifetimes to affect your world. I don't know what stories your legends tell, but I don't need you as a sacrifice."

"Not a sacrifice." The mouse twisted its tail in its paws and squeezed the dandelion-yellow puff of fur at the end. "A fellow journeyer. A participant."

Diamma grumbled, but then she said, "Mundo, are you hearing this?"

The turtle-elephant answered in her ear, "Bring the Snomoth mouse."

~

THE SNOMOTH MOUSE whose name was Eip rode across the snowfields behind Diamma's ear, clinging to the thick golden locks of her mane. When they entered the spaceship, the bright light dazzled Eip, and the warmth of the air embraced her. It was dizzying. She continued to ride the lion-lizard hybrid through passageways large enough to house skyscrapers, and then the passages opened into a chamber large enough to hold a small town.

Diamma grabbed Eip gently with a scaly talon, pulled softly until the mouse let go of her mane, and then set her down on a console beside a giant tank with clear walls, filled with a roiling, bubbling liquid. Anything else inside was obscured by the bubbles.

From her position on the console, Eip could see Aggem with his stately antlers and fearsome hooked beak working another control panel with his feathered arms. Like Diamma, Aggem was a giant compared to Eip.

A window behind the antlered-avian looked out on the familiar pale pink snowfields of Snomoth, but as Aggem worked the controls, the pink-blanketed countryside fell away. Azure clouds wisped past the window until they filled it. A few moments more, and the clouds cleared.

Although she'd felt no acceleration, Eip found herself looking down on her world from space. The sphere was white and swirly from the outside, luminescent like a pearl dropped onto the black curtain of space. Eip understood what she was seeing, because she'd seen photographs of Snomoth from space before; her people had withdrawn from interstellar society, but they hadn't forgotten what they'd learned.

As Eip's eyes adjusted, she saw the pinpoint diamonds of light scattered throughout the blackness. "Stars," she squeaked. "I've never seen them before."

"They're burning out," a nasal voice said.

Eip looked up to see another giant—this one had a wrinkly prehensile nose that extended from his face into an arm-length trunk, and a green shell curved over his back. In spite of a pair of tusks on either side of the trunk, this giant looked less fierce and predatory than either Diamma or Aggem. A twinkle in Mundo's eyes made the little Snomoth mouse feel inexplicably safe.

"I need to take your blood now," Mundo said, holding out the syringe with the end of his trunk.

Eip trembled as the needle neared her and let out an involuntary squeak when it pierced the skin on her arm under her fur. But it was over fast. Mundo truly drew only a drop of the mouse's blood.

Then the turtle-elephant laid the syringe down on a shiny patch of the very console Eip stood on. After Mundo pushed a few buttons with his long nose, the shiny panel under the syringe glowed with a blue light. The blue flashed several times, and then turned green before switching off.

Suddenly, previously dark screens all over the console lit up with rushing strings of numbers or letters in a language Eip couldn't read. The figures streamed by too fast to be deciphered even by someone who could read the language.

"The ship's computer is sequencing your genetic code," Mundo said, swinging his trunk rhythmically back and forth, as if ticking off the time while they waited.

"How long will it take?" Eip squeaked.

Diamma set her scaly green talons over the panel reverently and stared down at the streaming figures with wide gold feline eyes. The movement brought her large curving claws and sharp teeth much closer to Eip than made the mouse comfortable.

"Only a moment more..." Diamma purred.

~

AFTER EONS OF SEARCHING, putting together the puzzle gene by gene, constructing the genome of the final, most perfect chimera—the Inheritor of the Universe—there were only moments left.

Diamma felt Aggem's presence behind her; his feathered wing brushed against her scaly back. The antlered-avian had left the ship on auto-pilot, drawn with the rest of them to watch the final moments of the puzzle falling into place.

The translation of the mouse's genetic code ceased streaming across the panels and froze in place—a single gene highlighted in brighter letters. Of all the traits contained in the mouse's tiny body, this was the one that the final chimera lacked: a slight resistance to one of the rarest forms of cancer.

Stunned, Diamma said, "That won't visibly change the final chimera at all..."

"What did you expect?" Mundo asked, working the controls with his trunk for the birthing chamber that rose behind the panel, still thick with roiling bubbles. "We've been to hundreds of worlds, the three of us. Before that, we started with a computer bank containing the genetic codes for literally thousands of species from all across the universe—from at least a dozen galaxies."

"I thought—" Diamma started, but Aggem cut her off.

"This means we've already seen the final form. Essentially." He fluffed his wings, ruffling out all the feathers. "We just didn't know it."

Diamma felt like she'd been waiting to open a present, only to be told that the gift she'd been waiting for had been in her quarters, sitting on the bedside table in plain sight for several months already. Robbed... but selfish and ungrateful for feeling that way, because she'd gotten the present, hadn't she?

"I haven't seen it," the little yellow mouse squeaked from her place on the control panel. She was still wearing her heavy winter clothes; although they must have been far too warm inside the ship.

"Look behind you," Diamma said.

The little yellow mouse turned and watched the bubbles clear inside the liquid filled birthing chamber. As the liquid calmed, holo-emitters rendered a shadowy image of the final chimera inside the tank, faint and translucent like a reflection on glass.

The mouse didn't visibly react, but Diamma noticed that her round ears were standing very tall and her whiskered nose was twitching very fast as she processed the image in front of her.

A dozen heads sprouted from the creature's body like flowers from a bush—three beaked and feathered, five covered in varying shades and lengths of fur with muzzles of different shapes, two with glittering scales, one with smooth skin, and one covered in petals like a literal flower. From the creature's long back, six pairs of wings arched—two scaly dragon wings, three feathered wings, a pair of bat wings, and one pair of butterfly wings as beautiful and colorful as stained glass. Its multitudinous legs and arms were all different shapes and bends, but its tail was a single, graceful curve that narrowed down to a tufted end.

"It has a tail puff like mine!" Eip squeaked.

"Not much like yours," Diamma grumbled.

"The final chimera is a conglomeration of so many different species that it's impossible to see the individual affect of any particular species' genome," Mundo intoned, lecturing like an expert. Though he was no more of an expert than his two fellow researchers.

Diamma liked to imagine that the gold flecks in the left eye on the chimera's fourth head, one of the fuzzy ones with bull-like crescent horns, had something to do with her own golden eyes. It rankled her that this tiny mouse, a pure genetic species with a single planetary origin, saw herself more easily in the final chimera than she did.

And yet, every sentient species in the universe should see themselves in this most complicated of reflections. It was the mirror that melded all of them together.

"I can't do it," Mundo said, his trunk holding the lever that would start the materialization process. He played the role of their leader, but it was all youthful bluster and overconfidence.

The turtle-elephant hybrid was the youngest of the three crew members. He'd studied the birthing chamber, but he'd never seen it actually used, because the last time it was used was to materialize him.

Diamma and Aggem had designed Mundo and material-ized him in the birthing chamber after their last crew member —an insectoid giraffe with six very long legs—had passed away from old age. Before her, there had been a duckbilled platypus. Diamma remembered him fondly. He'd been like a father to her. When the duckbilled platypus had died, Diamma and the six-legged giraffe had designed Aggem who had come to be like a brother.

There were always three crew members.

Diamma was the oldest now. She'd be the next to die.

She grabbed the lever with her scaly talon and said, "I can do it." She didn't want to die like her forebears had, before the end of their mission. She wanted to see the universe fold in on itself, fulfill its final purpose.

She pulled the lever.

Bright lines of laser light—red, green, and blue—pierced the liquid-filled birthing chamber from every direction. At their intersections, the dots of light burned so brightly that Diamma immediately turned her head, closing her eyes. But the after-image of the final chimera glowed inside her closed eyes. For an instant, in bright primary colors, flipping a moment later to a negative afterimage clothed in eerie darkness. Satanic and troubling.

Diamma opened her eyes.

The light from the birthing chamber had dimmed. The lasers were still doing their work, intersecting with each other, catalyzing the soup of proto-cellular matter, inspiring amino acids to dance together, twist together into chains, and cut the final chimera from whole cloth—born fully formed by the magic of science. But the brightness of the lasers was now eclipsed by the physical presence of the chimera's body. It had mass. It had volume.

The final chimera stretched, twisting its long back.

It had never done that before. Never moved. It had only ever been an image, static and changed only by newly input data. A computer program.

Now it had life and could move by choice. Stretch a cramped wing. Scratch an itch behind an ear. Or turn one beaked face to stare at Diamma with eyes that sparkled with so many different shades of green, they could have been entire planets filled with rainforests, savannahs, and sea green waters. Whole ecosystems in a pair of eyes.

Time fell away, and Diamma knew she was looking into the eyes of her father, long gone though he might be, as well. Then reality twisted, and although her own eyes were gold and these were green, it was as if the universe itself had become a mirror and Diamma was sure she was staring into her own eyes too.

The chimera whipped its long tail into the side of the tank with a thundering crash. The glass wall shattered, and the birthing fluids rushed out, soaking the control panel and splashing to the floor. Eip was swept away by their waters, but

Diamma reached out to rescue the little mouse. She settled Eip in the locks of her mane again.

"What happens now?" Eip whispered in Diamma's ear, and the lion-lizard realized she didn't know.

For generations, a triad of chimeras had flown this ship from star to star, planet to planet, following a trail of breadcrumbs, genetic clues, baked into the fabric of the universe since the beginning of time. By the time that Diamma's quasi-parents, the six-legged giraffe and the duckbilled platypus, had constructed her, the mission was nearing its end, but she didn't know what that end meant.

"Our mission is over," Diamma whispered back, feeling totally lost for the first time in her life.

Diamma looked to Mundo, the most self-assured of the current triad, but he'd tucked his head so far back into his shell that all she could see of his face was his curled up trunk. He felt as lost as she did.

Diamma turned to see Aggem's reaction, but he wasn't looking at the final chimera standing in godly glory on the wreckage of the birthing chamber. Stretching its half-dozen wings, yawning its dozen mouths, testing its hooves and hands and paws and talons.

Aggem was looking back at the ship's viewscreen, and Diamma followed his gaze. On the screen, the planet Snomoth grew and shrunk, changing color and shape like the pictures in a twisting kaleidoscope. "It's every planet," Aggem cawed. "Every planet we've ever visited, all at once." It was like looking down a hall of mirrors—every image separate, but somehow all the same. Separated by time instead of space. Every planet was the same planet, no matter how it seemed to look, the truth of them was the same.

A dozen voices spoke in unison, each with a different timbre in a different language, but the voices blurred together, harmonizing into a clarion call, so bright in its clarity and meaning that it could have been etched into the very sheet music that the universe had been written on. "Now, we start new missions."

The final chimera held a paw out to Mundo, a talon out to Diamma, and a hand toward Aggem. When a god holds its hand out to you, you take it. When Diamma felt the final chimera's talon clasp her own, she felt a contentment deep in her belly that filled her until it spilled out of her throat in a rumbling purr.

"We will be the architects of a new universe together," the dozen voices said. The triad was a quartet, and their new symphony had just begun.

"What about me?" Eip squeaked. She had wanted to journey with the chimeras through this universe, but constructing a new one... The little mouse was totally out of her depth, and she knew it.

Twelve faces looked at her.

Twelve voices spoke:

"You will stay in this universe. It ends for us, but for you, it will go on. You will tell our story."

RETURNED to the pink snowfields of her home world, Eip watched the silver ship of the chimeras ascend through the clouds and disappear. Pink crystals, giant snowflakes fell softly in its wake, and tickled her whiskers. The small mouse shivered.

She had only been gone from her world for a few hours, but Eip had returned with a lifetime of purpose. She had a story to tell, a song to sing of the end and the beginning, swallowing each other, and looking into a god's many eyes.

ABOUT THE AUTHOR

Mary E. Lowd is a prolific science-fiction and furry writer in Oregon. She's had more than 200 short stories and a dozen novels published, always with more on the way. Her work has won three Ursa Major Awards, ten Leo Literary Awards, and four Cóyotl Awards. She edited FurPlanet's ROAR anthology series for five years, and she is now the editor and founder of the furry e-zine *Zooscape*. She lives in a crashed spaceship, disguised as a house and hidden behind a rose garden, with an extensive menagerie of animals, some real and some imaginary.

For more information:
marylowd.com

To read Mary's short stories:
deepskyanchor.com

For news, updates, discounts, and deals:
marylowd.com/newsletter

ALSO BY MARY E. LOWD

Otters In Space

Otters In Space

Otters In Space 2: Jupiter, Deadly

Otters In Space 3: Octopus Ascending

Otters In Space 4: First Moustronaut

Otters In Space Spinoffs

In a Dog's World

When A Cat Loves A Dog

Jove Deadly's Lunar Detective Agency (with Garrett Marco)

The Entangled Universe

Entanglement Bound

The Entropy Fountain

Starwhal in Flight

Entangled Universe Spinoffs

You're Cordially Invited to Crossroads Station

Welcome to Wespirtech

Beyond Wespirtech

Brunch at the All Alien Cafe

Xeno-Spectre

Hell Moon

The Ancient Egg

The Celestial Fragments (A Labyrinth of Souls Trilogy)

The Snake's Song

The Bee's Waltz

The Otter's Wings

Tri-Galactic Trek

Tri-Galactic Trek

Nexus Nine: A Tri-Galactic Trek Novel

Voyage of the Wanderlust: A Tri-Galactic Trek Novel

Commander Annie and Other Adventures

The Necromouser and Other Magical Cats

The Opposite of Memory

Queen Hazel and Beloved Beverly

Some Words Burn Brightly: An Illuminated Collection of Poetry

Furry Fiction Is Everywhere (with Ian Madison Keller)